Protecting Bria

A Forced Proximity Bodyguard Romance

TN Seal Security Nashville Division
Book 1

KeKe Renée

Chiquita Dennie

304 Publishing Company

Synopsis

A case that could make her career could also mean the end of it.

Bria

I'm finally making a name for myself. After years of law school, endless hours of studying and overtime, I've finally landed the case to put my career on the map. I just didn't realize the corruption and danger that would come with it, or that I'd be forced to stay with a bodyguard twenty-four-seven.

Cairo

As a Navy seal, my career has been my entire life. With only one case left, I'm ready to retire. But I didn't expect Bria. The smart, sexy, and completely naive attorney needs my protection. And now it's my job to keep her safe.

The fight is on.

Grab your copy of Protecting Bria now and indulge in a romantic suspense unlike anything you've ever read. If you enjoy military romances, damsels in distress, forced proxim-

ity, and steamy romance, then this is a series you don't want to miss.

Introduction

Grab some wine and get ready for spicier, sinful, sexy fun with Bria, Cairo, and the team from TN SEAL Security Nashville Division.

Are you signed up for my newsletter?

Join today and find out all the latest in new releases, contests, giveaways, sneak peeks and more.

https://BookHip.com/BKRPJL

Disclaimer

This work of fiction contains strong language and explicit sexual content and is only intended for mature readers. This story may contain unconventional situations, language, and sexual encounters that may offend some readers. If you're looking for sweet, fluffy romance, I would recommend another book. This book is for mature readers (18+).

Note To Readers:

Protecting Bria is re-relased from previously being published under another author's world. Same story updated characters, partner series of TN SEAL Security Series.

<u>**TN Seal Security Nashville Division Series**</u>

Protecting Bria TN Seal Security Nashville Division Book 1

Protecting Chanel TN Seal Security Nashville Division Book 2

Protecting Yanira TN Seal Security Nashville Division Book 3

<u>**TN Seal Security Series**</u>

Aydin: Book 1
Nasir: Book 2
Nicco: Book 3
Knox: Book 4
Vaughn: Book 6
Jasper: Book 7

Latest Releases

By Keke Renée:

Wet Heat

Every Time We Touch (A Wet Heat Novelette)

His Peace, Her Pleasure

Baby, It's Cold Outside

Love Don't Live Here Anymore (Andrew sisters) Book 1

Love Don't Live Here Anymore (Andrew sisters) Book 2

One Night Only-A Novelette

Deidra's Love

Haven

Seeking To Please

Seek To Touch

Seek To Bare

Seek To Love

Seek To Trust

Seek To Earn

Tease Me Book 1

Promise Me Book 2

Consume Me Book 3
Claim Me Book 4
Tempt Me Book 5
Ravage Me Book 6
Sensual
Protecting Bria (TN Seal Security Nashville Division Book 1)
Protecting Chanel (TN Seal Security Nashville Division Book 2)
Protecting Yanira (TN Seal Security Nashville Division Book 3)

Chapter One

Bria

I turned, facing the room. "Your Honor, Mr. Giovanni is guilty of destroying this city and should be convicted and sent to jail today. I rest my case," I said, staring into Moses Giovanni's eyes. He smirked, not fazed by my glare. Today was closing arguments in the People of New York vs Moses Giovanni, a notorious mob boss. This case had gone on for over seven months and multiple prosecutors have dropped out because of intimidation or judges who pushed the case back. Judge Bell was one of the toughest judges in New York because you never knew which way he would side. I was nervous when he was first assigned, based on some of my colleagues' past experiences with their cases being tossed out, dismissed from lack of evidence, or witnesses backing out at the last minute. Judge Bell picked up his gavel and called for a five-minute recess. The courtroom was full of reporters, fans of Moses Giovanni, and I suspected there were even a few cartel members sitting in the back.

I headed back over to my chair, gathering my documents to leave. No matter what happened, I promised the families of his victims that I would fight to get justice—either from seeing him in jail or working to get a civil suit filed.

"Bria, I suggest you leave this case alone. You're making a big mistake," Sean Lockton, the defense attorney, muttered in my ear.

"The mistake was you not taking the deal of life with the possibility of parole, Sean. Tell Mr. Giovanni how life is going to be when the announcement comes in that he's going down for destroying the local communities of this city," I spat back as Judge Bell walked back inside.

"All rise," the Bailiff announced. The courtroom stood, waiting for the judge to take a seat. Adjusting my jacket, I clasped my hands together in front of me, standing straight with my shoulders back.

"The case before me was overwhelming and enlightening with how things have transpired in the city of New York over the past few years. Mr. Giovanni, I can unequivocally say how your actions have caused many families to no longer feel safe where they work or live. In order to bring some sense of peace and justice to the city, I hereby find you guilty of ten counts of RICO charges. The next court date for sentencing will be decided in a month," Judge Bell announced. The courtroom erupted in cheers and boos. I peered over to Moses and the cocky smirk on his face caused a chill to race down my spine. His lawyer whispered in his ear as the police handcuffed him and led him out of the courtroom.

"Bria, can we talk?" Sean asked, following behind me as I walked out of the courtroom to leave for the day. Reporters stopped me on the front stoop as protestors shouted in support of Moses.

"Miss Dawson, how do you feel about the verdict?" the CBH reporter asked.

"I feel good about the verdict, and I look forward to the sentencing next month," I answered.

"Is it true that Mr. Giovanni had the chance to make a deal before going to trial?" she questioned.

"I won't comment on what the proceedings were, but Mr. Giovanni was treated just like any other defendant in a courtroom. No favors were given, and I can personally say I never took a bribe," I replied.

"What are you expecting from the sentencing? Are you working with the families on the civil suit?" she questioned.

"Again, I can't answer questions about any ongoing cases, you'll have to speak with the family. I expect justice to be served. Thank you, my time is up," I told her then pushed through the crowd.

Free Moses Giovanni! Free Moses Giovanni! the crowd yelled.

Getting through the crowd, I accidentally bumped into a hard chest. Glancing up, the word SEAL was inscribed on a man's vest. Feeling his hands around my waist I stepped out of his hold, clearing my throat. Embarrassed from staring at his bright smile, my body had a reaction I didn't want to admit to myself.

The last guy I dated, Kory, wasn't completely honest about his life and I fell right into his arms after needing someone to confide in about my career. Finally, after applying at so many firms and DA offices and being turned down, I got a position. I could still see the disappointment in my mother's eyes for not following in her footsteps at her firm as an associate. I wanted to make it on my own and my dad, a big-time doctor, was the one to comfort me whenever my mom and I disagreed about the choices I made. To her, getting married at the peak of my career would be foolish and was something she deeply regretted. I could tell by the way my parents behaved when they were around each other, their marriage was more about convenience rather than love. Grayson and Charlotte were the poster parents for the perfect family to the outside world. But to me, it was all a façade. This man in front of me would bring only pain and suffering I couldn't even bear to think about.

"Excuse me," I said and walked around him and the other guys wearing SEAL vests and guns. I stepped off the curb and opened a cab door when I heard a car screech nearby, then a window rolled down and an automatic weapon was pointed right at my head.

"Gun!" someone screamed from behind me, but I was frozen and couldn't move fast enough.

"Get down!" another voice yelled. All of a sudden, I was pushed to the ground by a heavy body as bullets ripped by our heads.

"Ahhh! OMG!" I screamed, coming out of my frozen state and covering my head. A few minutes later, the shots stopped and the huge guy hovering over my body leaned up and checked me for any wounds.

"You're safe. It's done," he said and I nodded, shaking in his arms. He stood and extended his hand to pull me up.

"Cairo, you good man?" another guy asked.

"Yeah, did you see who it was?" the guy named Cairo asked.

"The car had tinted windows. Nasir is getting Columbo on the license plate," the guy replied.

"I'm sorry, I'm Cairo and this is my teammate, Aydin. Though his nickname is Superman," Cairo told me, then reached out his hand for a shake.

"Bria Dawson, prosecutor. Nice to meet you both and

thanks for saving me," I replied, bending down and grabbing my briefcase. As I tried to walk away the police stopped me.

"Miss Dawson we can't let you leave," the police officer said, holding up his hands to block me.

"What's going on?" I asked. The court steps were flooded with police and medical personnel. I was fine, so there was no reason for me to stay.

"We received a tip that a hit was put out on your life. The drive-by shooting was meant for you, ma'am," he replied before speaking into his radio. The ambulance appeared along with more reporters.

"Who put a hit out on me? That's ridiculous!" I exclaimed.

"Moses Giovanni," the police officer replied. I looked around for Sean and saw him talking with a medic. Stalking over to him, I pushed my way through the crowd.

"Did you know?" I questioned.

His eyes narrowed in confusion.

"The shooting. Your client put a hit out on me," I announced and some of the reporters overhearing my statement tried to push their microphones in my face.

"What client?" Sean asked.

"Don't play dumb, you know I'm talking about Moses."

He got off the gurney and grasped my arm tight, pulling me out of earshot.

"Let go of me!" I shouted.

"Shush. Please, Bria, calm down," Sean replied, and I shook my head, crossing my arms over my chest while I tapped my foot.

"Are you all right?" I heard the deep velvety smooth voice behind me. I looked up to his face.

"Um. Yeah," I responded.

"Who are you?" Sean questioned, pointing at the guy who saved my life.

"Cairo Holden, SEAL team assigned to help escort a defendant," Cairo said, peering into my eyes but talking to Sean. This wasn't the time, but staring at his thick full lips, strong Romanesque nose, full beard, chiseled jaw, and dark brown skin had me wishing the circumstances were different. A man's eyebrows and lips were the sexiest things, and his perfectly trimmed brows and heavy-lidded eyes made me want to confess all my deepest, darkest secrets. Someone cleared their throat, making me blink out of my trance.

"Who ordered a SEAL team to escort my client?" Sean investigated, raking his hands through his hair.

"The mayor and governor didn't trust that the local police would be able to handle this alone, so they called us in to help," Cairo said.

"Did you know about this, Bria?" Sean questioned, and I held up my hands to stop him from accusing me of anything shady.

"Take it up with the mayor, Sean. All I know is that your client tried to have me killed. I think more charges should be added before he's sentenced. I bet Judge Bell would love to hear about this."

"Cairo, are you ready to go?" Aydin asked, and Cairo smiled at me before walking away. A sexy man that's tall at six-three was a dream come true. His dreads were pulled up in a bun on top of his head. I was kind of surprised the Navy allowed him to have his hair in dreads, but I knew nothing about military protocol. Regardless, he was mighty fine and I would hold the memory of how he was concerned for my safety close.

Chapter Two

Bria

I turned back to Sean as he pulled his cell phone out of his pocket.

"I don't know what games you're playing, Bria, but this isn't going to get you to the top as AG any time soon," Sean stated, stalking off back to the courthouse. I trailed behind to give him a piece of my mind.

"You have some nerve blaming this on me when *your* client tried to kill me."

"Miss Dawson is it true the drive-by shooting was aimed at you?" a reporter from GTC news asked.

"No comment," I replied.

"Mr. Muller, we have received word that it was done by your client, Moses Giovanni," the same reporter insisted.

"No comment!" we both spat out as we rushed inside toward Judge Bell's office. My body locked up when we walked in and the same men from earlier surrounded his office, sitting in the chairs in front of his desk.

"Mr. Muller, thank you for joining us. We have a little bit of a predicament," Judge Bell said, removing his glasses.

"Your Honor. I had no idea about any shooting at the courthouse. I would never participate in anything that would bring harm to anyone," Sean said.

"Mrs. Dawson—"

"It's Miss Dawson, sir," I said, glancing over at Cairo. Something told me to let this man know I was unmarried. Not even knowing if he was married or dating anyone, I couldn't understand the sense of urgency, but I'd learned to follow my instincts and made sure he was aware I was a free agent.

"Miss Dawson, did you see the face of the shooter?" the judge asked.

Shaking my head no, I replied, "I didn't, sir. Everything happened so fast I just froze."

"That's when I pulled her down on the ground, sir, and covered her as my team returned fire," Cairo explained.

"What do you think, Mr. Holden?" Judge Bell asked, standing up and grabbing his jacket.

"I think you should put a protection detail on her until he's sentenced and maybe around the clock at her home and family," Cairo stated.

I raised my hand, then asked, "I'm sorry, but what are you talking about?"

"Giving you protection, Bria. Obviously, whatever this is needs to be dealt with immediately and my wife is having surgery which means the sentencing, I'm afraid, is going to be postponed."

"I'm not the only one working this case. Why is he targeting me?" I asked, eyes widened, pacing back and forth while hugging myself.

"Until we know for sure what his goal is, we need to keep you safe. Aydin and his team come highly recommended by the AG and governor. Sorry to say, kid, but you just became Moses Giovanni's number one enemy," he informed me.

"He can't have this much power. He's a criminal that's killed and robbed people for over five years or more."

"I understand your frustrations, Bria, but you asked for this life and it doesn't come easy," he advised. The room went quiet and I sighed, taking a seat in the chair next to Cairo.

"If we know he's put a hit out, can't you attach the charge and do the sentencing today?"

He shook his head. "No evidence it was him, this is all hearsay at the moment. If we bring it up, the repercussions could backfire, and you need to move smart."

"Judge Bell, my client wouldn't do something like this," Sean insisted, and I scoffed at his statement before jumping up and pushing him in the chest in frustration.

"You knew, didn't you?" I shouted as anger churned in my chest.

"Bria! Calm down...*Bria!*" Sean barked as he shoved my hands away, causing Cairo to jump up and slam him against the wall, gripping his neck. The one I knew as Aydin tried to talk Cairo down as the Judge yelled for him to let Sean go.

"Don't you ever put your hands on her again," Cairo gritted through his teeth.

Sean held his hands up in surrender. "I'm sorry, it was an accident. Bria knows me," he pleaded, out of breath.

"Cairo, let him go. He's not worth the headache, bro," Aydin murmured, placing his hand on Cairo's shoulder. Sean looked relieved when Cairo loosened his grip.

"Apologize," Cairo demanded, folding his arms over his

chest. Sean cleared his throat while he fixed his suit jacket. I was surprised that the judge who's normally 'by the book' didn't say anything about Cairo roughing up Sean.

"Bria I...I apologize, I didn't mean for any of this to happen."

"I know, Sean, it's okay," I replied, trying to ease the tension in the room. Glancing at Cairo I nodded a thank you, then picked up my briefcase to leave.

"Can I go now? I have to call my parents," I asked.

"Cairo is leading your protection detail while we're here in New York. Normally, we're based in Memphis and their team is in Nashville, but my wife is here for work and we got the call about this mission. I know it seems scary, Bria, but you'll be safe with us," Aydin responded, opening the door of the judge's chambers.

"Keep me updated and tell the Commander to call me when he gets more information," Judge Bell said as everyone walked out. Cairo held a file folder and passed it to another guy who hadn't been in the office with us.

I started to head outside to leave but Cairo held out his arm to block me.

"First rule when you're with me. You'll never open a door when in my presence," Cairo said, pushing open the door then letting me go first. I stopped on the first step and turned.

"How long do you think this will last? I feel like my life is going to be interrupted with all of this protection. I mean, what if I have a date?" I joked.

"We're not here to interrupt your life, Bria, just to keep you safe. Also, if you have a date, our IT guy will need to do a background check on him before you can go out," Cairo answered.

I reeled back in shock. "You're kidding, right?" I questioned, then planted my hand on his chest before he could walk off.

"No, I'm not. I take my job seriously. Before, we thought this was simple transport, but now it's turned into a protection job. I was ready to retire today, but you're not the only one that's having a bad day," Cairo said.

Chapter Three

Bria

H e walked off toward a row of red Dodge trucks as more men stepped out and shook hands with him.

"I know this is a huge disruption to you but we'll try our best to stay out of your way," Aydin said.

"Should I call you Aydin or Boss? I don't want to get in trouble for saying the wrong thing."

He chuckled, then stated, "Aydin is fine. Cairo isn't so bad."

"Was he really about to retire?" I asked.

Aydin nodded. "After doing three tours and working as a SEAL for the past five years, he's ready to retire at thirty-five."

"Who are the other guys?" I pointed to the men Cairo was talking with near the trucks.

"Knox, Jasper, Nasir, Bishop, and the rest of my guys are back in Memphis," Aydin answered as he escorted me down the stairs.

"Wait, Knox, Nasir, Bishop, and Jasper?"

"Jasper is the flirt of the group same as Bishop, Nasir is

more friendly amongst us. Knox is the funny guy, but always there if a job needs to get done. Then you have Cairo *Chase* Holden, my second-in-command when I'm not around."

He opened the passenger door for me, and I asked, "What does Chase mean?"

"Ask him." Aydin chuckled, closing the door. I watched Cairo shake hands with his team and walk around to the driver's side, getting in and putting the file folder in his lap, then start the car and pull into traffic.

* * *

Forty-five minutes later we pulled up to my house in New Jersey. Cairo turned off the car and I started to open the door.

"You don't listen, do you?" Cairo asked, shaking his head. He climbed out and trekked to my side of the car, opening my door.

"Sorry. I can take it from here," I insisted, the thought of my nosy neighbors asking questions about all these cars in front of my house and it getting back to my parents worried me. I couldn't imagine how they're going to feel when they saw the news about the attempt on my life.

"We have to search the house," he said.

"That's ridiculous, Chase." I bumped into his chest when he stopped abruptly and turned.

He reared back. "What did you call me?"

"Chase. That's your SEAL name, correct?" I questioned.

"I'm going to kill Aydin," he grunted, stomping to my front door.

"It's not his fault, he was telling me about all you guys. Bishop, Jasper, and the rest," I said, passing him the key.

Aydin strolled over with two more men. "Bria, this is Maddux and Soaquan. Bishop's in the car," Aydin said, following Cairo inside while the other two went around to the backyard.

My house was in a quiet suburb with mostly families and a few younger people—one being my best friend, Alana, who lives three doors down and works as an executive assistant to a photographer.

We met in high school and now at thirty-three the both of us are in the prime of our lives and careers. However, having our own homes and being single had its own set of problems.

"You have a nice home, Bria," Aydin said, bringing me out of my thoughts.

"Thanks, my parents gave it to me as a graduation gift from law school," I replied, dropping in the chair next to the couch and kicking off my shoes.

"All clear back here, Aydin," Maddux said, walking in from the back door.

"Cairo, we'll leave Knox and Nasir here as backup. I have to go pick up Amelia from this work thing. I'll be at the hotel if you need me," Aydin informed him, patting Cairo on the back and shaking hands with Jasper.

"Maddux, can you work with Columbo and get a trace on Moses' close contacts? We need to know who he called over the past few days to get the ball rolling."

"Bria, right?" Maddux asked.

"Yeah."

"Don't give my brother a hard time, I saw you two arguing on the steps. He means well even if he doesn't come across so well," Maddux said, winking at me.

"You take every moment to flirt, don't you?" Cairo lifted his right eyebrow in question.

Maddux and I chuckled at his reaction.

"She's a beautiful lady," Maddux replied, picking up my hand and placing a kiss on the back.

Cairo pushed him toward the door and scowled at me.

"He's a big flirt," I said, jumping up to head to the kitchen.

"Maddux is a good guy, but a flirt. All of the team is great," Cairo said as he walked into the kitchen.

I opened the fridge, grabbed a bottle of water, and motioned to Cairo to see if he'd like one. Taking it out of my hand, he unscrewed the top then sipped it slowly as our eyes made contact.

"So, tell me about yourself, Cairo, since we'll be around each other for the next thirty days or so," I said, taking a seat at the kitchen table. He motioned to me as if to ask if he could have a seat and I waved him over.

He held out his hand. "Cairo Holden."

Sliding my palm inside of his large hand, I found it surprisingly soft.

"Bria Dawson."

"Nice to meet you, Bria, and yes I had it all planned out to have my feet up on my boat drinking a nice cold beer."

"You don't live here full time?" I asked, removing my suit jacket and leaning back in my chair.

"I don't, but I have a home in Hendersonville, Nashville, as well as Hawaii," he answered.

"What does your wife think about you being here every few months?"

"Single, what about you?" Cairo questioned, gulping the rest of the water bottle. Huh, guess he didn't hear me in the judge's chambers earlier after all. Standing up, I walk to the fridge for some space and pick up my phone.

"Ordering pizza, are you allergic to anything?" I asked.

Chapter Four

Cairo

I saw her before the shooting started. We'd been in the courtroom for the past few weeks as she argued the case. Bria was bad for me in all the worst ways. Her cute heart-shaped lips, sparkling deep-set hazel eyes, and ebony brown skin made for one hell of an attractive package. When she was in the courtroom, I noticed the way she owned the witnesses during the cross examination. During the discussion in the judge's office she seemed so innocent and doe-eyed. I couldn't pinpoint when I started to see her in a different light. I wouldn't call it feelings because bringing a woman into my lifestyle as a Navy SEAL would be too complicated. I'm really surprised Aydin and Amelia have gone so long, considering they met when he ran into her at a time she needed help.

"Hello, Cairo! Cairo!" She snapped her fingers in front of my face, bringing me out of my trance.

"Sorry, I'm fine with anything," I answered.

She nodded, giving her address and disconnecting the call.

"I'm not married and don't have kids. I'm thirty-five, in

the prime of my life, and my mom is constantly wanting grandbabies whenever she finds out I'm dating. She'll probably ride my ass until it happens," I joked.

"Is it because you're off traveling a lot? The job seems dangerous."

"Partly. My job is very demanding and the women I've dated hated being second place in my life," I told her.

"I understand a demanding job. Being a lawyer in New York brings out the craziness in men. They can't handle a woman that has her own money and doesn't need them for anything except a good orgasm," she said, shrugging. The doorbell rang and she started to stand up but I stopped her from going to the door. I know Maddux probably checked the person, but I wanted to do an extra follow up. Opening the door, a kid no more than eighteen years old was shaking while holding two pizza boxes. Maddux and Bishop were on either side of him.

"Delivery...for...you...sir," the kid said, passing me the boxes. I turned to Bria giving her the food as she scowled at Maddux and Bishop.

"Thanks, kid, here's a hundred. Keep the change for the stress they put you under," I said, shaking my head at them as they stepped inside.

Maddux rubbed his hands together, taking a seat on the couch.

"Did you two have to scare him?" Bria argued, dropping the napkins, pizza boxes, and water bottles on the table.

"We only scared him a little, doll face. Better us than Chase here," Maddux joked, pointing at me.

"Tell me how you got the nickname Chase?" Bria questioned, her eyes crinkled in mischief.

I groaned, running a hand down my face. Bishop and Maddux burst out in laughter.

"I guess you can say I'm good at chasing criminals down," I answered.

She took a bite out of a slice of pizza, and I watched as sauce dribbled on her white shirt.

"Darn it, I need to go change," she said, jumping up and heading toward her room. Her place was a one story, brick-modern style. I had a condo in the city I rented out. But my place in Hendersonville is two stories on ten thousand acres. I'd just put in a basketball court, grill, and pool in the back. I went to Hawaii after a case to relax. Since most of my SEAL brothers lived in Memphis and Nashville, it was home.

"She's cute," Bishop mentioned.

"Get it out of your head," I commented.

Soaquan chuckled, then stated, "It's true."

"Chase, you have to admit this assignment isn't all bad in the grand scheme of things," Maddux suggested.

I waved him off as Bria walked back into the living room wearing long jogging pants and a white tank top. Clearing my throat, I licked my lips and watched as she offered the guys something to drink other than water.

"How old are you, Bria?" Maddux asked, winking at me.

I furrowed my brow and flipped him off.

"Thirty-three," she answered.

"Married, kids, any history of mental illness?" Maddux inquired.

She jerked back in shock, then asked, "What is this, an interrogation? I'm not the one on trial, Maddux."

"Sorry, doll face, a habit of mine," he said.

"Ignore him, Bria, we're like that when we meet a new person," I said, jumping into the conversation to smooth things over.

"For your information, yes, I'm single and have no kids. My parents wouldn't even want me to have kids until my career is established."

"You do everything your parents say?" I asked.

She shrugged in answer, so I changed the subject.

"What can you tell us about Moses? From the information we've gathered, he's a narcissistic asshole with too much power."

"He's the son of the legendary Michael Giovanni, a retired mob boss who still has ties within the political system. I think the only reason he was caught this time was because the people around him dropped the ball."

"How high up do you think? I mean, for him to set up a shooting in front of the courthouse is bold and sends a message," Soaquan wondered.

"From reading his file, they put people on payroll from the jail, possibly the Mayor's office," I stated, passing over a few documents.

"You don't think they'll do anything at my house, do you?" Bria inquired.

"I wouldn't put it past him. If we have a breach, then we'll move to a hotel. I think you should stick to your normal routine and not veer away from it. Hang with your friends, call your parents. Keep it simple, it'll draw them out."

"I don't want to put my friends and family in any danger," Bria said.

Maddux and Bishop looked at each other and then at me. They both stood up, took their trash in the kitchen, and walked out the front door. They'd stay in the car and keep watch.

"Bria, I want to be honest with you. Not to scare you but to keep the lines of communication clear. It's the only way we work as a team."

She groaned, throwing her hands on top of her head. I didn't want to tell her that the hit was set up a few weeks ago, but they kept it from her, and it was the main reason we were here on top of escorting him to Memphis where more charges were pending.

"Tell me," she said.

I stood up, captured her hand, pulled us toward the couch, and plopped down. She tucked her legs underneath her, putting distance between us.

"Judge Bell told me that this could possibly go on longer than one month. The more charges we can get on Moses the better. We think he's going to get a pardon if we keep him here in New York." She tried to jump up and I pulled her back down on the couch.

"So I'm a guinea pig! This whole thing is putting me and my family in danger. My father's a doctor and my mom is a lawyer. You can't be around them all day and night," she argued, crossing her arms over her chest.

"True, but my team will be here. Maybe they can take a vacation or something until it blows over. Judge Bell and I think this is the best way to catch everyone involved."

"You and Judge Bell can go to hell," she muttered, shaking her head in annoyance. I watched as she stalked off.

Taking my phone out of my pocket, I messaged Aydin.

Me: I told her the truth.

Aydin: I take it she's pissed?

Me: Beyond pissed.

Aydin: Give her some space.

Me: You know I don't do well with an angry woman.

Aydin: Amelia says hi.

Me: Tell her I said hello.

Aydin: I'll bring her by tomorrow so she can meet Bria.

Me: Does Amelia know?

Aydin: Yeah and she wants to talk with Bria in person.

Me: So I'll have two women mad at me?

Aydin: Lol! It won't last long.

Me: All right, talk tomorrow.

Aydin: Don't stress Chase.

I closed out and went to see if I could apologize to Bria and grab a blanket and pillow to sleep on the couch.

I headed down the hallway and knocked on the third door to the right, hearing music. Knocking a little louder, the door swung open and Bria stood in only a robe with a towel on top of her head.

"Sorry to interrupt. I wanted to grab a blanket and pillow to crash on the couch," I said, peering from her head to her toes. I thought she was sexy in a tank top and jogging pants, but she took my breath away standing in front of me right now.

"Uhm, they're in the hallway closet behind you." I

moved to the side and she opened the door next to the bath-room and grabbed a gray blanket and a pillow.

Taking both out of her hands, I said, "Thanks. I didn't mean to make you mad, Bria. If it's the last thing I do, your safety is my most important job."

"Cairo, I understand you're just doing your job. But this is a lot to take in and deal with. I'm putting my life in your hands."

"The team has always gotten the job done. You'll meet Amelia tomorrow, she's familiar with all of us."

"Let's just hope I live to see the sentencing."

I shifted, not wanting to continue the building tension between us, and went back to the living room. I tossed the sheet and blanket on the couch before I kicked off my shoes and laid my gun next to the pillow. I double checked the locks on the front door then headed to the back door to do the same while also closing the blinds. I checked that the guys were still outside and watched as they blinked the lights on and off in a signal that all was good.

As I laid on the couch I checked my phone for any messages. I set my alarm for seven am to let the guys in so we could do recon. I wouldn't be fully asleep thanks to my long Navy tenure. We're trained to always be aware of our surroundings, and any little noise would wake me. I didn't like to use my gun except as a last resort, my hands were lethal weapons by themselves. Drifting off to sleep, all I could hope is that it would be smoother tomorrow.

Chapter Five

Bria

I was sitting in my office, eating breakfast with Alana before she went to work at the studio. Cairo told me that I would be meeting Amelia today for lunch, so I wanted to get as much work completed as I could beforehand.

Alana passed me the vanilla almond latte and I took a sip, letting it simmer in my soul.

"So tell me what's going on with you?" Alana asked, crossing her legs and taking a bite of her vegan wrap.

"I know you saw the news and social media about the case I'm working."

She nodded in answer.

"Well Moses was found guilty and after the verdict I left, then someone tried to kill me."

Alana dropped her food on the plate, covering her mouth with her palm. "Oh my God! Bria, why didn't you tell me? I would have come over sooner."

"Everything happened so fast I didn't get a chance to call you. I still need to call my parents and let them know what's going on."

"Is that why you have that guy standing outside your office?"

"Yeah. His name is Cairo Holden. He's a Navy SEAL."

"He's cute. Does he have any friends?"

My mouth twisted in anger; I felt a lump get caught in my throat. *Was I jealous?*

"I only know the other Navy SEAL guys. I don't know if they're single or not, but Aydin is married to Amelia."

"Aydin? That's his real name?" Alana asked.

"Yes."

"What do you think your parents are going to say?"

I sighed, thinking of how that conversation would go when my mom heard about my situation.

"I can imagine this fucking up a dating life," she said, laughing.

I rolled my eyes at her comment and retorted, "I'm not worried about my dating life, Alana, someone is trying to kill me."

There was a knock on my door and Cairo stepped inside. Alana looked over her shoulder, then stood, extending her hand for a shake.

"Hi, Alana Clarkson," she introduced herself.

"Is something wrong?" I asked.

"A Kory Dickson is here to see you."

Alana and I made eye contact. Kory was my ex-situationship that had been on and off for a year. More off than on because our work schedules were demanding.

"You can let him in," I replied.

"What could he possibly want?" Alana asked.

I stood up, coming around the front of my desk as Kory walked inside with Cairo behind him.

"I'll be fine, Cairo, Kory's harmless," I said, waving him off. He nodded and left my office.

"Alana," Kory said, and she rolled her eyes. They had never gotten along.

"What can I do for you, Kory?" I questioned in an effort to get him out of my hair before Cairo thought something was going on between us. Having thoughts of keeping Cairo from thinking I was involved with someone seemed strange to me. Kory pulled me in for a hug. I reciprocated just to be nice.

"Kory, shouldn't you be at work or something right now? I mean with the amount of excuses you had for Bria last time you were in her presence I could be a millionaire now," Alana pushed.

"Alana, worry about yourself and leave my name out of your mouth," Kory spat.

"Okay you two. Alana, can you give us a minute please?"

"Don't fall for his lies. The sex can't be worth the headache," Alana bit out before throwing her trash away.

"Alana!" I shouted and Cairo opened the door, glancing at us. I didn't think my shouting could be heard but based on the hard glare on his face I might have opened a can of worms.

"Is there a problem?" Cairo questioned as Maddux walked inside, crossing his arms over his chest.

"Who is this, Bria, and why did I need to wait to be allowed in your office, babe?" Kory questioned, making it seem like we were together.

"Don't call me babe. We haven't been around each other for at least six months or more." I blew out a breath. "What can I do for you?" I clasped my hands together.

"Can I talk to you alone? It's private... Please, Bria?" Kory asked, giving me puppy dog eyes.

"Cairo, I'll be okay. This won't take long."

"Yeah, Cairo, let her fall down the rabbit hole with Kory again. I'll buy you and your sexy friend here a cup of coffee at the cafeteria. Oh, by the way, I'm Alana," Alana said, extending her hand to Maddux's.

"Maddux," he replied.

"Maddux? I like that. Does it mean you'll play my body like a *Mad Max* movie?" Alana flirted, biting her bottom lip.

"Alana, really?" I chastised.

"Alana's a sexy name," Maddux stated, sliding his hands in his pockets.

"Maddux, I just got a text from Aydin, let's wait outside. He should be pulling up," Cairo said, pulling him away from Alana as she chuckled then followed behind them.

Kory wrapped his arms around my waist, holding me to him. "What's up with the bodyguards?"

"You know the case has gotten out of control with the hit on my life," I said.

"What can I do to help? I miss you, babe," Kory said, leaning down and kissing my cheek.

I jerked back. "You miss me, or you miss the power couple status we had together?"

He groaned, then replied, "Don't start that, Bria. We were good together. You changed up on me."

"It's not about changing, Kory, it's about knowing what I want out of life and you're too self-involved to see outside of yourself. I'm not my mother and I won't have the type of relationship my parents have."

"Your parents have been married for over thirty years. Everyone looks to your parents as the couple to be. You're pushing away what could be a beautiful thing," Kory pleaded.

"That's funny because you always complained about

my schedule and not being the homemaker that you saw yourself marrying."

He sat on the edge of my desk, rubbing his beard.

"I don't knock you for what you want for yourself. I just can't see me staying home waiting on you hand and foot, Kory."

"We were good together, Bria."

"In *your* eyes, not mine. I have somewhere to be. Is there anything else you need?"

Wanting to end this back and forth conversation, I grabbed my coat and purse to head out for lunch. He bolted upright and tried to stop me from leaving, pushing his tongue into my mouth. I jerked back, smacking him across the face.

"Kory, it's over. Please leave me alone. Stop calling, dropping by, and contacting my parents. I've moved on," I explained.

Kory scoffed. "It's never over, Bria. You'll see what we have is worth fighting for."

"I doubt that," I said.

Cairo glanced over his shoulder as Kory walked out and I shook my head to leave it alone.

Maddux stood with Alana whispering in her ear before she walked left and he came near Cairo.

"I'm ready for lunch," I announced.

"Are you sure you're okay?" Cairo asked.

"It's just a past situation that doesn't need to be restarted. Kory's all about status and being the *it* couple. Something my parents keep pushing me towards."

As we stepped outside of the building a crowd of photographers surrounded us.

"Bria! How are you coping with the attempt on your life?" a reporter inquired.

"Bria! Bria! Can we get an exclusive interview on your life under protection?" a second photographer asked.

Cairo rushed me through the crowds with Maddux on my other side, both of them intent on protecting me and keeping the media vultures at bay.

"Keep your head down, Bria." Maddux said.

"Maddux, text Aydin. We should meet Amelia at the hotel instead of the restaurant," Cairo said.

My phone rang. Seeing my mom's name across the screen, I picked it up as the door closed on the truck.

"I know, Mom." I spoke first, trying to calm the situation before it got ugly.

"Bria Dawson, what is going on? I have two men outside my office and your father called saying some Navy SEAL men are following him around because some mobster put a hit out on you," Mom said.

When Charlotte Dawson was pissed you'd never live it down.

"I was going to call you, but things moved quickly after the verdict."

"Come to the house, I'm heading there now," Charlotte commanded.

People banged on the truck as flashes went off. Maddux pulled into traffic with Cairo in the passenger seat. Bishop and Soaquan were behind us in a second truck as backup.

"I have a meeting I'm heading to right now," I informed her, holding my hand over the end of the phone.

"Your meeting can wait. Your parents are more important," Charlotte spat out before hanging up.

"Alana said she'll call you later. She had to head to the studio," Maddux told me.

"I'll call her later. Can we make a detour to my parents' home?"

The car stopped at the red light.

"How far is your parents' place from the Hilton Hotel?" Cairo asked.

"They live on Long Island."

"That's an almost two-hour drive," Cairo said after checking his watch.

"Text Aydin that we'll be late. You need to meet your future in-laws," Maddux joked, and

Cairo smacked him on the back of the head.

"Thanks," I said as Maddux turned right and headed toward my folks' place. To the public we were a well-established family that traveled in high profile circles. Not staying with Kory was a slap to their faces, well, at least to my mother's. Father didn't really care for my ex, but he never challenged her in front of me. I was just trying to find my place and dealing with this case would be a struggle, but I felt it was right to see it through the end. I closed my eyes, preparing myself to deal with my mother's contempt about the way I lived my life.

Chapter Six

Bria

The car was silent as Cairo texted back and forth while Maddux sped down the highway. Eventually he pulled into my parents' driveway.

"All right, we're here," Maddux said.

Seeing both cars in the driveway, I counted to five to calm my nerves. Charlotte had a way of pushing my buttons.

"Let's get this over with," I said as Cairo and Maddux opened the door. Bishop arrived and waved. I waved back, climbed the stairs, and knocked on the door.

"Why didn't you use your key?" Cairo asked.

"When you meet my parents, you'll understand."

The door opened and my father smiled, reaching out for a hug. He kissed both of my cheeks and pulled back, smiling at me. I loved my father, but he was the quiet type who let my mother run the family and never really disciplined me or argued against her rules.

"Bria, sweetie, so good to see you. Come on in and tell us what's going on. Your mother's been on a rampage since this morning when she called me at the hospital," Dad said.

"Dad, this is Cairo and Maddux. They're my protection until the sentencing," I replied.

My dad extended his hand for both men to shake, and Maddux and Cairo took turns doing so.

"Thanks for finding the time to grace us with your presence," Mom stated. Maddux closed the door behind us as we sauntered to the couch.

"Can I explain before you start yelling?" I asked.

"No because once again you've left your father and I out of your life and now we have this sprung on us. Do you understand the clients I deal with?" Mom questioned.

"I know, damn it! This isn't my fault," I snapped, rubbing my forehead.

"Who do you think you're talking to, young lady?" Mom demanded.

"You! My *God* can you let me breathe for a second?" I shouted, then stomped toward the kitchen to grab something to drink. Dad trailed behind us down the hall.

"Charlotte, hear her out," Dad insisted, pulling her down on his lap.

"Ma'am, you can blame the lack of communication on me. I told Bria to wait to contact you. My name is Cairo Holden, her protective detail on her case," Cairo explained.

"I told her to do business entertainment, hell even family court. This is interfering with my job," Mom replied.

"Charlotte," Dad muttered.

"No, Grayson, this case is all over the news and the papers. My clients are scared to work with me until it's over. I'm losing money because she wants to save the world from some gangster," Mom responded.

"Um, Mrs. Dawson, I don't know your daughter that well but what she's doing is a great thing. Saving the city from people like Moses Giovanni and his associates is a good thing," Maddux said.

"Which one are you sleeping with, Bria?" Mom asked.

My mouth dropped open in shock.

"Neither if you must know. And by the way, Kory came to my office today. I gather it was on your insistence to try and get us back together," I said, standing in front of her and my father. Cairo tried to pull me back and I shook him off.

"Kory is the type of man you should be dating and marrying. You're not getting any younger, sweetie. Men like them will only bring drama into your life," Mom advised as she pointed toward Cairo and Maddux.

We watched her walk out of the room, leaving all of us in shock.

"Give her some time, sweet pea," Dad said.

"I'm constantly being patient and respectful and silent. Tell your wife I'm done trying to play up to her public image," I stated before walking out the front door.

"Bria," Cairo called out, stopping me before I could get the door closed.

"No, Cairo, you see what she's like. It's all about her and no one else matters," I said, heading for the truck.

"Bria!" my dad shouted.

I walked toward him and he met me halfway.

"I'll talk to your mother. You know she loves you and I can admit I didn't do much when you were growing up as I let her lead the family. But she wants you safe just like I do," Dad said, kissing my forehead.

"I know, but she needs to stay out of my life and let me make my own mistakes. Also, stop calling Kory to try and get us back together. I've moved on."

"Is it with the Cairo fella?" Dad questioned.

I reared back in shock. "What?"

"When you were talking to your mom, I could see the way he was looking at you."

"Dad, he's only here to protect me and nothing else."

"Okay, sweet pea," Dad replied, pecked me on the cheek, and ambled back inside.

...

After a disastrous afternoon with my parents we finally got back into the city to meet up with Aydin and his wife, Amelia.

Cairo led the way into the restaurant of the Hilton Hotel and pointed to a table with Aydin and a woman I assumed was his wife. Once we were at the table they both stood up and I waved for them to take a seat.

"Hi, I'm Amelia," she said, extending her hand for a shake.

"Hi, Amelia, nice to meet you. I'm Bria."

"Have Aydin and the team been nice to you? I know these boys can get into a zone when they get around each other," Amelia commented.

I nodded in answer to her question.

"Amelia, don't start please," Cairo said.

I looked between the group and they snickered at his statement.

"Let me guess, you gave Aydin the nickname Superman?"

"I gave it to him when I first met him when he kind of saved my life a few years back," Amelia replied, sipping her water.

"Wow! What was the issue?"

Everyone looked at Aydin.

"Nasir and I kind of found her by accident one night. Amelia happened to be a surprise I didn't know I needed."

"Seriously?" I questioned as the waiter came over and handed me a menu.

"Hi, I'm Kendall. I'll be your waiter this afternoon. Is there anything I can get you to drink?"

"Your number," Maddux answered, smirking while Kendall blushed.

He really was the biggest flirt I'd ever seen. I wondered if Alana gave him her phone number.

"Just water and salad for me please," I answered. Amelia ordered a burger and fries, as did Aydin.

"Is there a Bria Dawson here?" Kendall asked. I pointed to myself and she passed me a note.

"So, what do you do, Bria?" Amelia inquired.

"I'm a lawyer, well a prosecutor for the state. You've probably seen my face plastered on all the news stations lately."

"I don't watch that much TV as an office manager," Amelia said.

"That has to be exciting."

"It is, but some people think it's boring. I've seen the most exciting things over the past few years in my line of work."

The waitress brought our food and we continued to talk and get to know each other for the rest of the evening until I remembered the note.

Unfolding it, I almost threw up at what was written. A photo of my home showing the door broken in and the inside ransacked had been attached.

Dear Bria

You may think you're protected, but we have contacts in all places. Don't get too comfortable Miss Dawson.

Address: 2345 Lambert Street New York, New Jersey.

"What's wrong?" Cairo questioned, taking the note out

of my hands. I jumped up to leave but Cairo pulled me back down.

"Damn it!" Cairo shouted, slamming his hand on the table.

"Is it him?" Aydin asked.

Cairo passed him the note.

"Maybe you should stay here at the hotel," Amelia suggested.

I grasped Cairo's hand. "Oh my God! What about my parents?"

"They'll be fine, I will send Bishop and Soaquan to watch over them. Columbo has eyes on them already."

"This is all my fault," I said, wiping the tears falling down my cheeks.

"Who gave you this note, Kendall?" Aydin questioned, scanning the room.

"A gentleman that was over by the hostess stand. Did I do something wrong?" she asked.

"No, it's not you. My men need to get a description of the guy. Maddux can you take her to the back and I'll text the guys to see if anyone saw anything strange from the car," Aydin said, pulling out his phone.

"I really don't want to stay in a hotel," I admitted.

"What about staying with Cairo at his condo?" Amelia suggested.

Chapter Seven

Cairo

Everyone lost their appetites at lunch, so Aydin moved Amelia out of the Hilton and to a hotel closer to my condo. Maddux and Soaquan were in the same hotel as them and we agreed that it was better if Bria stayed with me until the sentencing phase of the trial was over. We went back to her place to grab a few of her things and called the police to file a report about the break-in. One of my contacts who owned a repair shop put in a new lock and deadbolt. When she talked with her parents, they told her everything was fine on their end and she explained she'd be staying with me since she wasn't comfortable in a hotel.

Opening the door, I flicked the lights on and placed her bags on the floor. The condo was more of a bachelor pad, and with me being in Nashville more than I was here I hadn't really decorated. The living room held a simple couch, a TV, and a few pictures on the wall.

"Make yourself at home. I know it's not much, but I usually only stay here a few months out of the year."

"Ooh. Are you sure it's okay for me to stay here? I don't

want to impose on you, Cairo. I mean you've done enough and if something happened to you, I wouldn't be able to face your family."

"My parents understand the work that I do, and they live a few miles from me."

"Are you one of those guys that has women running in and out by a certain time so they don't bump into each other?" she probed.

I chortled, removed my holster and vest, then placed them on the kitchen counter. My condo was an open space with the living room and kitchen as one giant room. I had two bedrooms and two bathrooms with a deck on the back.

"Ask me what you really want to know, Bria," I said, kicking off my shoes and grabbing a water out of the fridge. She leaned over the counter, watching me as I stood against the stove with my arms beside me.

"Tomorrow I want to visit Moses in jail," she said, changing the subject.

"I don't think that's a good idea."

"I have to confront him. Maybe I can get him to confess about what he has planned for me, and we can end this before it gets dangerous for everybody."

"Do you trust me?" I questioned.

"It's not about that, Cairo." She sighed, moving to sit in the chair near the fireplace.

"Moses is the type of man that thrives on riling up his enemies."

"I know that. I've spent months working this case after other people dropped it because they were too scared or got paid off," she told me.

"That should tell you he doesn't care *who* you are. Let us do our jobs and we'll figure everything else out. You can sleep in the guest bedroom."

I headed down the hallway and left her in the living room to sit with her thoughts about what I'd said, hoping she would leave it alone. I placed my gun on my nightstand, then grabbed a T-shirt and boxers to take a shower so I could finally rest. Tomorrow Aydin and the team wanted to do surveillance on Moses' people, and I planned to have Amelia sit with Bria to keep her company while we were gone. Alana wanted to know where she was staying, but I didn't trust anyone and told her that if Bria wanted to see her we'd meet her in the city. I prayed Bria listened to me and didn't go behind my back and try to do things on her own. Maybe I should have Soaquan or Bishop stay with the women.

* * *

We drove to one of the clubs that Moses owned. I left Bria at the condo, while Amelia was close by at a meeting, then she'd swing over in case she needed anything while we were out. Aydin wanted them to get together afterwards when she's finished.

"This is the place," Maddux said.

"Club Luxx," I muttered.

Maddux pulled out his gun and checked the chamber.

"No shooting," I told him.

"How did Bria sleep?" Aydin asked.

"Fine. She wanted to go visit Moses in jail. She thought she could convince him to let up."

I slid open the door of the club and we walked inside as loud music played. Thankfully, it wasn't too crowded since it was eleven in the morning. A few women were dressed in shorts and sports bras with the word *Luxx* written across their chests. I stepped over to the bar.

"Hey, fellas, we're not open until one," the bartender said.

"This isn't a social visit. I wanted to ask you a few questions about Moses Giovanni," I replied, showing my badge.

"I can't help you," the bartender stated, then turned to walk off.

I grasped her hand. "I believe you can. What's your name?"

Her eyes shifted around cautiously. "Look you can't be here. You'll get me in trouble with my boss."

"I'm Cairo, and you are?" I reached out for a handshake.

"Crystal," she answered.

"Crystal, this is Aydin and this is Maddux. I promise we'll keep you safe."

She looked around the club, then murmured, "Hurry up and ask me before Albert comes out here."

I peered at her and asked, "Albert's the manager?"

"He's the underboss and cousin of Moses," she responded, wiping down the counter.

Aydin and I glanced at each other.

"How long have you worked here, Crystal?" Aydin inquired.

"Long enough to know that I could get killed for talking to you," Crystal said, folding the towel and placing it under the counter.

"Albert run things now that Moses is locked up?" I asked and she chuckled.

"Moses runs things, Albert is just the face of the Cartel. Moses will be home soon," she replied as the door opened and two men dressed in suits and wearing black shades walked inside.

"Crystal, who are your friends? The club isn't open yet unless Albert made an exception," one of the guys said.

"I was just telling them we aren't open, Diego," Crystal replied.

"Gentlemen, do you need an escort out?" the guy named Diego asked, putting his hand on my shoulder.

"I think we can find our way," I said, turning to leave.

Diego laughed as Maddux and Aydin followed me. As we got to the door Diego said, "Tell your little girlfriend anything can happen during a jail visit."

I turned around and grabbed him, jerking him up by his collar.

"What the fuck did you say?" I gritted out.

He took a swing, hitting me in the right side of my stomach. I dropped my hand from his neck and returned a hit to his jaw. Aydin pushed Albert back before he jumped in and we went blow for blow.

"Son of a bitch!" Diego groaned.

A gunshot went off and we stopped. I looked up to see a guy no taller than five-seven, his hair in a bun, with small beady eyes and thin lips surrounded by a mustache, wearing a light gray suit.

"This is private property. If you don't leave, I have the authority to shoot in self-defense," he smugly stated, a sneer marring his face.

Diego wiped the blood off his lips.

"Who are you?" he asked.

"Tell Moses I'm coming for him," I replied and marched back toward the car with Maddux keeping an eye on my back.

Starting the car, I backed up, turned the wheel, and pulled out of the parking space. I grabbed my phone out of my pocket and dialed Bria's number.

"Amelia's not picking up," Aydin said.

"Bria isn't either."

"Let me try Soaquan," Maddux stated.

He placed the phone on speaker, it rang twice before he picked up.

"Maddux, what's up?" Soaquan asked.

"Soaquan, is Bishop there with you?" I yelled.

"Yeah, what's wrong?"

"Go upstairs and check my place. Bria and Amelia aren't answering their phones," I said, pushing the gas to seventy miles an hour as I rushed through traffic.

"Fuck!" Aydin shouted.

"We've been here all morning, no one has come in or out without access to the building," Bishop remarked.

"I have a funny feeling about this," I responded as I swerved in and out of traffic, honking my horn and flipping people off.

In no time I made it to my place and turned off the car, jumping out immediately. All three of us rushed inside and instead of taking the elevator we took the stairs two at a time to get to the fourteenth floor. I had my gun locked and loaded when I saw Soaquan and Bishop walking out.

"They're fine, Cairo," Bishop said, holding up his hands.

"Where are they?"

He pointed to the back hallway and I saw Amelia come out in a robe drying her hair. Less panicked, I put my gun away and watched Bria swish through nonchalantly.

"We already know, don't be upset," Amelia said, wrapping her arms around Aydin and kissing his lips.

"You had us all worried, babe, you can't go off without letting us know," Aydin responded.

"The pool called our names and Bria needed a break from being cooped up," Amelia said.

"Sorry, I got off the phone with the District Attorney and they want to put me on leave until this blows over. I guess word got out about the break-in at my place," Bria commented.

"That's still no excuse to not answer your phones. The only way this works is if you listen to me, Bria." I grimaced as I stomped over and got in her face.

"My life is already a mess, sorry if I wanted a few minutes of peace without the noise of the outside world." Bria huffed, biting her bottom lip.

"You don't think I know that?" I shouted back, pointing at my chest.

Bria shook her head in annoyance.

"Cairo, let me talk to her," Amelia said.

"Please, someone talk some sense into her head," I barked.

I attempted to walk off but Bria grasped my arm and shouted, "Fuck you, Cairo!"

Chapter Eight

Bria

My blood pressure was through the roof. After Cairo left this morning my job informed me I was on leave, and then my mom called with Kory on three way trying to set us up again. Today had just been unraveling nonstop and then to have Cairo bust in here and yell at me like I was a child... I was ready to leave and get someone else to be my detail.

"What happened to your face?" I asked, finally noticing the bruise on the side of his jaw. I grazed his cheek and he jerked back in pain.

"It's not as bad as it looks," he replied.

"Aydin what happened?" I walked to the fridge and grabbed an ice pack, placing it on his bruise.

"We went to a club that Moses owns and ended up meeting Albert, his underboss," Aydin answered.

"You think he's the one that's running the show now?" I asked, picking up my briefcase and file folders on the Giovanni Cartel. I had a few items from the office that I kept in case of emergencies. "I have a safe at my office and I keep a few files as backup, right now is the main reason for the safe because clearly I can't trust everybody. Is this Albert?" I held up a photo of Albert and Moses talking in front of his nightclub. Cairo took it out of my hands.

"Cairo was able to talk to the bartender, maybe we can get her to work with us to take Albert down," Maddux chimed in, looking at the photo.

"When does the sentencing happen?" Amelia questioned.

"Thirty to thirty-five days. The judge's wife is having surgery," I replied.

"Bria, I need to tell you something," Cairo said. My stomach turned at the hesitation in his voice.

"What is it?"

"The team was put in place to monitor the trial. Columbo is working to take down Judge Bell, Albert along with the whole Cartel operation and I couldn't tell you earlier."

"Wait, so I've been arguing a case in front of a judge that's in cahoots with trying to get me killed." I was struggling to stand. Cairo tried to help me, but I pulled out of his grip.

"We should talk about this later," Cairo stated, and I shook my head.

"Tell me the truth, I need to know."

* * *

Flashback four months ago.

The courtroom is filled to maximum capacity and standing room only. It was the fifth day of the trial and Sean questioning a witness that paid Moses a fee every month to keep his business from being destroyed like other mom-and pop-stores.

"Mr. Jacobson. Can you tell me what this so-called fee includes?" Sean asked.

"Safety and protection from rival gangs—and Giovanni gangs," Jacobson replied.

He was the third witness I had prepared to take the stand, and now he fell apart in front of everyone.

"Objection, your Honor." I drilled Sean with a glare while he walked back to his seat, shaking hands with Moses.

I pulled on my jacket and counted to three in my head to control my temper and push through the bullshit day I was having.

"Mr. Jacobson, you spoke with me about the money you have to send monthly to Moses Giovanni, correct?" I stood next to the jury box, watching him squirm in his seat.

"Yes," he answered, wiping the sweat off his face.

"And originally this wasn't a protection fee like he's doing you a favor, correct?"

"Leading the witness!" Sean shouted.

"Let me rephrase. You were in the middle of having your business burned down unless you paid Moses ten thousand dollars."

"I don't remember," Jacobson replied.

"Would you recall if I brought in your wife?" I asked, clapping my hands together, standing with my shoulders straight back.

"You promised that—"

The judge banged his gavel.

"Mr. Jacobson, yes or no answers," Judge Bell said.

"Again, Mr. Jacobson, you came to us and explained that the block your business is on has to pay ten thousand dollars to keep it safe."

"Yes, that's true," Jacobson replied.

"That will be all for this witness, your Honor," I said,

looking up and noticing a pair of eyes staring back at me. He held a stony glare, but had a sexy face that commanded attention. I shook off the trance I was in and stepped back to my chair.

"Your Honor, I would like to call Albert Giovanni," *Sean announced. The doors opened, and a group of men walked inside, going to the section with Moses' family.*

The memory replayed in my mind.

"Albert was a surprise witness that day in the courthouse, but there was nothing substantial to make Judge Bell worry," I told the group.

"Yeah, that day he walked inside. We were there, and you noticed us in the back. It was the day we got our orders from our contact to stay close," Cairo informed me.

I pulled out everything I had on Moses, Judge Bell, and the rest of Moses' family.

"We should order some food," Amelia said.

"You're going to the hotel to rest. I'm not sure how long this will take, and I already felt like my heart was beating out of my chest when we couldn't get in touch with you earlier." Aydin linked their hands together and brought her in close for a kiss on her lips.

Amelia broadened her stance, wrapped her arms around his neck, standing on her toes, and kissed him deeply.

"All right, but can you call me when you're on the way to the hotel, so I don't worry?" Amelia insisted, and Aydin smiled, squeezing her close.

"Amelia, we can do lunch tomorrow since I'll have more free time," I said.

"That will be fun. You can meet me at work, and we can go from there," she responded, trekking over and giving me a hug bye.

Even though we'd just met, she'd become a good friend.

"Aydin, don't forget." Amelia held her hand in the gesture of a phone next to her ear.

Aydin opened the door for Amelia to walk out first to leave.

"Tomorrow, we can call Victor with the FBI to get a clear understanding of how far up this goes," Aydin stated.

"Look at these phone records. I hadn't gotten them traced yet," I said.

"Columbo," Aydin and Cairo said at the same time.

"You think he can get it done in time?" I asked.

"He's the best in the business," Aydin said.

"Moses isn't married, and the last I checked he takes his women to a hotel when he wants to be alone with them."

"He has to have one that's consistent," Cairo said.

"Most of the photos have him alone or with Albert," I replied, standing up and heading to the kitchen.

"I wonder if the club has surveillance video that Columbo could tap into," Cairo said, his eyes following me as I opened the fridge and grabbed leftover pasta.

"That's a good idea. I'll message Victor and Columbo tomorrow," Aydin stated.

"Are you guys hungry?" I asked, pulling four plates from the cabinet.

"I could go for food," Maddux answered and rubbed his stomach.

I glanced at him over my shoulder. "Maddux, are you telling me your women aren't feeding you?" I teased.

Maddux lifted my palm and kissed the back of it. "No one as beautiful as you, Bria," Maddux flirted.

"Maddux!" Cairo barked.

Maddux and I looked between each other, and he winked at me.

"Yeah, Chase?" Maddux replied.

"I need you to do some recon on the Judge tonight," Cairo said.

"And miss dinner with my new friend Bria?" Maddux complained, and I chuckled, waving him off.

"I can send you a to-go plate with Soaquan," I answered, and Cairo grunted. Maddux and I burst out in laughter.

"He's not that bad, Bria, just a big teddy bear and territorial," Maddux informed me.

"Not sure I'm his type."

"Don't let what happened with Kory define the rest of your life," Maddux suggested, and I agreed as he walked out of the kitchen and left the condo with Aydin. Cairo came over and stood in the archway of the kitchen with his hands in his pockets.

I turned with my back to him and could feel his eyes staring holes in the back of my head.

"Dinner will be ready soon."

"I was worried about you," Cairo whispered in my ear.

Chapter Nine

Bria

Turning, I'm met with Cairo's hard chest. He licked his lips, staring down at me. "I'm attracted to you, Bria."

"Okay."

"But we can't act on those feelings," he replied.

I cleared my throat, moving a piece of hair behind my ear. "Why?"

"I made a promise to myself that I would never get close to a woman that I worked with because the type of work I do causes unnecessary drama."

"Aren't you retiring? I mean, we both have demanding jobs."

"I *was* retiring. Now that Albert is aware of the team, we can't sit this out and leave you out in the open," he said.

I turned back around to plate our food and wiped my hands on a paper towel.

"So, tell me about your parents," I said, changing the subject.

"Maddie and Thomas Holden live close to me and seem

to think they're still young going out more than me." Cairo chuckled, sitting down in a chair near the kitchen table and watching me prepare dinner.

"How so?"

"All my life, I've been able to be free around them and not feel like I was a child that needed to stay in my place. They instilled trust, communication, and unconditional love in our house."

"Something I wish I had with my parents, or at least that my father would call my mom out more."

"She loves you," Cairo said, looking up at me. I smiled back, and the smell of bread wafted in the air. I had made Alfredo with red sauce, and Amelia brought over red velvet cupcakes, so sitting out by the pool was a relaxing experience to let everything else escape my mind.

"My mom means well, but she has a hard way of proving it to me."

"They didn't want other kids?" Cairo questioned.

"No, they barely wanted me. I was an oops baby." I laughed as I picked up the large wooden spoon to scoop the food out of the pan.

"What do you mean?"

"One time my mom and I were arguing, and she let it slip that I wasn't even planned. She didn't know until she was around four months pregnant. Dad begged her to have me." I remembered the cold shoulder my mom bestowed on me for a week.

Cairo whistled, rubbing his beard.

"I take it they like Kory for you?" Cairo took the plate out of my hand.

"Our parents wanted us together because it would look perfect for our family status."

"Why did you two break up?" Cairo bit into the bread.

"He wanted a woman to stay home and take care of the house while he worked. Plus, he wanted me on his arm for social events."

"Has he contacted you since that day in your office?" Cairo questioned, putting the fork down and peering at me.

"Besides when my mom tried to do a three-way call with us? No, and I didn't tell him about me being on leave from work or that my place was broken into."

"Good," Cairo said. He jumped up, grabbed his plate, tossed the leftover food away, and then washed his dishes. I was impressed that a man like him even knew how to do something so basic, but I found I liked that he did.

The rest of the night, we talked and read through the files I had on Albert and Moses and how they took over from his father and the local gangs that worked under them.

* * *

Days passed and Cairo and Aydin were driving Amelia and me to my parents' house. They'd requested to see me and Cairo wasn't letting me out of his sight. I remembered driving in and out of the city to Long Island because my parents wanted to keep me away from the dangers of city life as a teenager. Alana used to come and stay with me for weeks during the summer and that made the time go by faster. Most of our friends were at the clubs or had been dating once they hit sixteen and had their own cars. I didn't get my own car until I was twenty-one when I bought it for myself.

Bang!

I screamed, covering my head. Amelia and I sat in the back, and more shots went off.

"Get down!" Cairo shouted.

"Amelia!" Aydin screamed.

"I'm okay, Aydin," Amelia told him as we crouched down.

Bang!

The side mirror was shot off as Cairo swerved in and out of traffic.

"Who is that?" I panicked, looked behind me, and saw a black van behind us.

My eyes enlarged as a gun was pointed right at me. I ducked as the back window shattered.

Cairo tapped the Bluetooth on the steering wheel, and Bishop's voice came through.

"We're on them, Chase," Bishop replied.

"Stay down, you two!" Aydin demanded, leaning out of the window and sending shots back to the van.

Amelia and I were sunk low in the seats as bullets went back and forth. All of a sudden, the car tilted.

"Bishop! We're going down!" Cairo yelled, attempting to keep the car from driving into another car as everything went black.

* * *

Hearing voices, I slowly opened my eyes and noticed Amelia, Aydin, Bishop, and Maddux in a group huddle. My mom was sitting in a chair reading. To my right, Cairo was asleep in the small chair next to the hospital bed. I tried to raise up, and the monitors went off.

"Hey, doll face," Cairo stated, caressing my cheek.

"What happened?"

"Bria, you're awake, thank God," Mom said.

"Amelia, are you all right?" I asked, running a hand over my forehead as the door opened and my dad trekked inside.

He captured my hand. "Sweet pea, you scared us."

I adjusted in the bed, slowly, and winced. "Sorry."

"What happened?" Mom inquired.

"We were on our way to your house and was ran off the road," Cairo said, leaving out the shooting.

His hand slipped into mine and squeezed.

"We did a CAT scan, and nothing major was damaged, but I want you to stay overnight and get rest. You took a bit of a tumble," Dad stated.

"Are these doctors' orders or my dad talking?" I joked, trying to ease the pain.

He glanced at the monitors. "Both. I think you should stay with us when you get out of here."

"She's good with me," Cairo said.

"Obviously not if she's being run off the road."

"Ma!" I snapped, not wanting to hear her bitch.

"Mrs. Dawson, I trust Cairo with my life, along with my husband and his team. This won't happen again," Amelia stated, taking up for Cairo.

"Cairo has taken good care of me, and his condo is safe," I said, trying to break the glare as she stared at Cairo.

A knock sounded on the door and Soaquan opened it as Kory walked inside with a bouquet of flowers. I groaned, watching my mom smile and kiss Kory on the cheek.

"Babe, I heard what happened. How are you feeling?" Kory questioned.

"What are you doing here?"

"I called him," Mom answered, taking the flowers out of his hands and strolling toward the bathroom to put them in some water.

"Thank you for the flowers, but you shouldn't be here."

"I thought we were going to tell your parents we're talking again," Kory lied, grinning.

"I never agreed to that," I spat, trying to sit up more comfortably in the bed.

"You heard her. You can go," Cairo demanded.

"I'm talking to my fiancée," Kory replied.

I jerked back in shock and, in a strangled voice, stated, "Kory, don't let my mom gas your head up. She doesn't run my life."

"Bria, give him a chance to make it right," Mom said.

"Dad, can you please take your wife out of my room?"

She reached for my hand. "Bria!" Mom screamed.

"Charlotte, let's go to the cafeteria. Bria's right, you need to stop meddling, and Kory, if I was you, I'd leave it alone and find someone else."

"Bria—" Kory started, but then Cairo reached over the bed and punched him in the face.

"Get him out here," Cairo commanded, attempting to hit him again.

"Are these the type of people you're dealing with, Bria? Shootouts, car crashes, and attempted murder on your life because of your job!" Mom shouted, pointing her finger in my face.

I called for the nurse, and she came inside as chaos erupted all around me.

"Can you please escort them out?" I motioned to Kory and my mom.

"Of course. Mrs. Dawson, I need you to leave," the nurse said.

Her lips pressed in a thin line. "Watch your mouth, little girl. I will own this hospital if you touch me," Mom snapped.

"You can leave with your husband, or I can have security escort you out. Your choice."

Kory grabbed his suit jacket and walked out as my mom rolled her eyes and left the room. Imagining the arguments that would take place once I was released was already causing me anxiety.

"We'll be outside waiting," Aydin said, captured Amelia's palm, kissing the back of it, and left Cairo and me alone.

"Did they get the men that caused the car crash?" I asked.

Cairo sat on the edge of the bed, caressing the top of my head. "You don't have to worry about them."

"Please tell me they didn't get away." I tried to get out of bed, and Cairo stopped me, gently nudging me back down.

"They're dead, Bria."

"Is this ever going to be over? I mean the number of enemies I'm fighting from Moses to Albert to the judge," I muttered, tears pooling in my eyes.

Cairo pulled me into a hug.

"You're not fighting alone. I'm here too," he said, lifting my chin and peering into my eyes. I grasped his chin, kissing his lips. I was tired of running from my feelings.

He stopped us from going further. "Bria, we can't do this."

"I'm sore, not dead, Cairo. A kiss won't hurt me," I replied then attempted to kiss him again.

He turned away from my lips. "No, I mean, us kissing. You're still dealing with old wounds from your relationship with Kory, and we both know our jobs are too demanding for us to lose focus by getting involved."

His thumb rubbed across my bottom lip.

"Stop pushing me away," I whispered, taking his face in

my hand and sticking my tongue in his mouth. He groaned, wrapping a hand around my waist. The heart monitor went off as we fell into our desires, and the nurse busted in the room.

"Do you need anything, Bria?" she asked.

I waved her off to leave us alone.

* * *

Back at Cairo's condo, Amelia came over to hang out and watch a movie with me while Cairo talked with the bartender again. The police showed up and asked questions about the crash and took our statements. Cairo suggested we keep it to a minimum and not give too much away because they could be on Moses' payroll or even the judge's.

"So, you kissed Cairo in the hospital?" Amelia asked, passing me the bowl of popcorn.

I took a handful and tossed the pieces into my mouth.

"I did, and I don't regret it one bit, but he's been cautious with me, and I wonder if he feels guilty."

"Try to keep those fears out of your mind. I went through the same thing with Aydin. He was feeling a push-pull with getting involved with me. At the end of the day, it's about your heart and not listening to your head sometimes."

"Did you fight your feelings for Aydin at first?"

She smiled. "It was more not communicating our feelings and thinking that he wouldn't see me in that light."

"What do you mean?"

"You're gorgeous, Bria, and I know you can have any man at your fingertips. As for me, guys just looked through me, and I felt Aydin wouldn't be attracted to me," Amelia confessed.

"Amelia, you're the most beautiful woman I've ever seen, and you're down to earth. Aydin is a lucky man to have you."

"I know that now, but back then, I felt like the odd girl out. I even challenged Aydin, Nasir, and Jasper about not really seeing me when we crossed paths."

"Well, I can tell you from the way Aydin looks at you, you're his whole world."

Chapter Ten

Cairo

Bria was still slowly getting back to herself after the car crash. Amelia called and checked in on her as much as possible, but she didn't want to worry anyone and tried to do everything on her own. I carried the tray of food into my bedroom and placed it on the night-stand. She paused the movie she was watching and looked over at the tray and tried to peek inside. I slapped her hand away.

"No peeking," I sassed.

She smirked, reaching her hand out for me. "Thank you for taking care of me, even if it is your job," she said as she caressed my cheek.

Clasping our hands together, I peered into her eyes. "This is more than a job to me, Bria."

"Cairo—"

I leaned over, placed a gentle kiss on her lips, and tried to move back, but she planted both hands on my face, pulling me in close.

"Bria, we can't, baby. You're still recovering." I admonished myself when my dick swelled in my pants.

"Please, Cairo, I'm fine, I promise."

I kept shaking my head, not wanting to pursue anything since I knew she was still hurting.

"You won't hurt me." She moaned and pulled me on top of her.

I groaned, thinking of the promise I made to myself that I wouldn't ever get involved with a client. Things could turn out bad if feelings got involved. Either they didn't understand the pressures of the job, couldn't handle the traveling, or they worried you'd get killed. Lifting up, I ran a finger across her bottom lip. I grinned and stood up, removing my shirt, shoes, and pants. Taking the condoms out of my wallet, I laid several on the bed.

Pulling the covers back, I asked, "You planned this?"

"What do you mean?" she teased, running a hand up my chest and down to my boxers as I stared at her in only a pair of panties and a thin T-shirt. I needed to control my hunger for her.

"These little ass panties you're wearing, and I can see your nipples poking out through this thin shirt..."

She opened her legs wider. "Then punish me," she murmured, her voice a whisper in the night.

"You're beautiful baby," I said, rubbing up and down her thigh. Bending down, I kissed her, then lowered my mouth and skimmed my lips along her cheek. I sank against her body, and my dick stiffened at the contact.

"Please Cairo..." she moaned.

Kissing down her chest, I tore at her T-shirt, engulfing her breast in my mouth.

"Fuck!" she cried out.

I drew a hard breath, switching between her left and right breast. The first time we kissed in the hospital, I wanted to take her then but knew it would be too soon. She clawed at my back as I thrust, feeling the hot sensation covered by our undergarments. My dick twitched as her hand came between our bodies and she gently ran it up and down my length.

"Cairo."

"Bria, tell me you really want this because once I get inside of you, I'm not sure I can stop."

"I want you."

"Lie flat on the bed." I dipped my nose in her essence, then ripped her panties away. Bria looked at me and shuddered in my hands as my mouth dove into her warm, sweet sex. Bria gripped the back of my head, pushing me closer. I pressed a hand against her leg, biting the inside of her thigh.

"Shit," I groaned, lowering my boxers.

She wiggled her hips, stroking the back of my head. My tongue darted in and out of her swollen sex.

"Ahhhhh!" she screamed, her juices dripping down on the sheets.

Her breath came in short pants, and I looked up at her, watching her body sink deeper in my arms. I hovered over her, curling one hand around her neck, the other anchored on her hip.

"Grab the condom," I said.

She hurriedly reached over, picked up the condom, sheathed my dick, and I lined myself up with her sex. Sliding in slow, trying not to hurt her further, I felt a sense of safety and love I'd never experienced before. This was new for me, something I never knew I was looking for.

"Uhhh... Bria baby."

The noise drowned out the thudding of my heart. All I heard was our low moans. Releasing her leg, I slid my hand to her head, my fingers tightening in her hair. Bria took my other hand, bringing it to her lips.

"Yes! Ohhh, please," Bria cried out.

"So beautiful, Bria," I said, kissing her lips, jaw, forehead.

I teased her nipple, biting and licking before moving back to her mouth.

"Mmmmm...Oh God!" She nipped and tugged at my mouth with a boldness that surprised me.

"Fuck Bria. Not God, baby. What's my name?" I challenged.

Bria arched her back, meeting me thrust for thrust.

"Cairo! Yes. Please," she exclaimed.

I shook my head. "When we're in here, open, vulnerable, and loving to each other, I want you to see me as Cairo not Chase, a bodyguard or anything else," I explained.

She begged for more, gripping the sheets as our scents tangled together.

"Fuck! I'm coming," I said.

Every muscle in my body weakened at the sight of her glow. Bria's sex pulsed as she slid her hand over my stomach and up my chest. The feel of her thighs spread around me as lightning flickered at my nipples from her touch had my balls drawing up.

"Am I hurting you?" I questioned, checking to make sure I wasn't putting all my weight on top of her.

"No, stop worrying and fuck me."

My head spun from the sensation of her pussy tightening around my dick.

"Stop that... *shit*," I said, filling up the condom and falling on top of her as she moaned, biting my ear as she came. I rolled off of her, then she leaned over me, grabbing another condom and removing the old one. Bria straddled my lap, slid down, put her feet straight ahead, and rode me for the rest of the night.

Bria was still asleep when my phone vibrated later that night. Removing her from the heat of my arms, I bent down and checked the multiple messages from the team.

Chapter Eleven

Bria

I was running on a high after the night with Cairo. Our chemistry was beyond my wildest thoughts as we orgasmed together. I was able to step out and hang with Alana today for lunch as long as Maddux and Abe were with me. At first, I wanted to push back but thought that it wasn't a good idea to start our situation with arguing. Even though I had strong feelings for him, I didn't want to be the first to admit that I cared. I couldn't say we were in a full-blown relationship. Maybe I was just a job for him. Bishop and Maddux sat a table over from us, wearing shades and ordering food. We were on the patio at our favorite place. Camille's was a restaurant between Cairo's condo and the stores so afterward we could shop for a new wardrobe.

"You look like you have a glow," Alana said, walking up to the table.

I stood up, reaching for a hug. She wore her normal all-black tights and large sweater dress and hat with minimal makeup.

"How are you?" I asked, trying to change the subject as we sat down.

The waitress came over after giving Maddux and Bishop their drinks.

"Hi, welcome to Camille's. I'm Nora, your server. What can I get for you?" she asked, taking the booklet out of her pocket to write down our order.

"Can I get tea and the usual BLT, fries, and fruit salad?" I replied.

"Sounds good. Anything for you?" she asked as she turned to Alana.

"I'll have the same and a piece of chocolate cake that we can split later," Alana stated, passing over the menu. Nora took them out of our hands and walked away.

Alana rolled up her sleeves, cupped her chin, turned her head to the side, and narrowed her eyes, trying to read my demeanor.

"Stop looking at me."

"You had sex," she whispered.

I rolled my eyes, not ready to have this conversation.

"That's rude."

"I tell you about my men, so tell me about Cairo. That's the one you're interested in, right?"

"He's protecting me on the case, and I was barely able to get out of his condo with everything going on, plus the car wreck," I told her.

"I know, why didn't you call me when you woke up? I could have been there for you."

"Sorry, I was just annoyed with my mom and Kory showing up. It was too much," I said.

"What did Cairo say about Kory?"

Nora came back with our drinks and fruit salads. I

grabbed the straw off the table and took a sip as she walked away.

"Nothing besides wanting to kick his ass."

"I wish I could have been there for you, babe. Work has been crazy for me."

"How is that going and your dating life?" I inquired.

"Work is picking up for my boss, and he wants me to start setting up European shoots for him."

"I'm happy for you. You've always wanted to travel with your job."

"I do, but this guy I'm seeing is driving me crazy and not wanting to go public with us," Alana confessed, taking a bite of her sandwich.

"Who is this guy? You're always mysterious with this one, compared to the others in the past that you dated and what about Maddux," I questioned, watching her top lip turn into a smirk.

"Maddux is just a flirt, a little fun. The guy I'm dating is not important, but I want to know how things are with you and your mom and this case. After the shooting and the car wreck, you went MIA," Alana stated, then wiped her mouth with a napkin.

I tossed my head back in annoyance.

"Mom's the same as she's always been. Think she knows how to run my life. I'm thirty-three, Alana. It's time for her to focus on her own business," I snapped. Losing my appetite, I pushed the plate away.

"Then tell her that and mean it this time. You said she wants you back with Kory, right?"

"That's never going to happen."

"Good because the two of you always fought about the littlest things."

"I have about another hour before I have to get back to

his place. Do you want to go with me?" I asked, standing up and putting forty dollars on the table for the bill.

"Okay, did I say something wrong? Your mood changed," Alana questioned.

I waved her off, locking my arm underneath hers as we stood at Maddux and Bishop's table. "You're good, girl. Let's go back and watch a movie or something. Gentlemen, you remember, Alana, my best friend," I said, pointing toward her as they reached out to shake her hand.

"We meet again, pretty lady," Maddux said.

"I remember that smile," Alana said, flirting and biting her bottom lip.

"We're ready to head back to Cairo's place if you're ready," I told them, breaking the stare-off.

"Sure, he should still be out with Aydin taking care of some last-minute details on the case," Bishop replied.

"What details are they following up on?" I inquired.

"Something about the car crash," Bishop remarked.

We all left the restaurant and headed to the car. I hoped he wasn't getting into anything too dangerous. Twenty minutes later, we made it back to the condo, and I made popcorn and opened a bottle of wine to watch one of Alana's favorite movies, *Coming to America*.

Chapter Twelve

Bria

Cairo stood underneath the water staring at me as his hand slid down to grasp his dick. I licked my lips, wanting a taste. The first time we made love, he wouldn't allow me the pleasure and not that I haven't tried, but he was so busy working the case that our alone time has been scarce.

I removed my robe and pulled my hair out of the rubber band, letting it fall down my back. He opened the shower door and reached his hand out to help me inside.

"I thought you were still asleep," Cairo said.

I grinned, wrapping my hands around his neck, standing on my tippy toes, and biting his bottom lip. Pulling back, he lightly smacked my ass, and I drove my tongue inside his mouth. Grabbing the backs of my thighs, Cairo lifted me up, and my legs automatically locked around his waist. I swallowed tightly as his dick eased in, filling me to the hilt.

"Ohhh... God!" I screamed as our bodies joined together to make beautiful music. His hot breath warmed against my ear as his pleasure drew nearer.

"Bria, I promise to protect you forever," Cairo grunted out, pumping into me. His arousal was weakening me from the inside out.

The pounding of my heart finally quieted at hearing those words from the man I thought I was falling in love with. I wanted to scream out that he belonged to me. His strokes deepened, and my eyes were heavy from the intense, passionate ache between my legs. The nearness of him gave me comfort and protection.

"I know, baby. Fuck me harder," I commanded, and he turned our bodies underneath the showerhead. Leaning away from me, he tightened his hands around my waist, thrusting faster. I held onto the door handle to steady myself.

"Ahhhhh! Yass! Right there... Mmmmm."

A guttural sound came deep from within his throat.

"Damn... Doll face come with me." Head tilted back, his eyes closed as we both met our orgasm together. Opening his eyes, his gaze met mine then zeroed in on my breasts. I giggled as he leaned over, kissing and massaging my breasts.

"The water is getting cold."

Cairo chuckled, reached around me, shut off the water, and put me on my feet. Picking the towel off the top of the shelf, I wrapped it around me and walked out, drying off. In his bedroom, I picked up the lotion and started to moisturize my arms. Cairo took the bottle out of my hand and motioned for me to take a seat. I sat on the edge of the bed, watching as he squeezed a little in his hands, before he bent down and lifted my leg over his shoulder, as he rubbed the lotion around my hips and thighs.

"I thought I drained you from the shower," I teased.

"Nope, I'm just getting ready for round two."

Cairo winked, pushing me flat on the bed, then he took more lotion and rubbed across my stomach. He licked his lips, then slowly slid his tongue inside my wetness. I flinched from the slight soreness, but his tongue turned me toward another orgasm.

"I swear your moans drive me insane." Pushing my legs farther apart, he guided himself inside me and shattered me into a million pieces. This was Cairo letting me know I was his and he was mine. He slammed into me, sliding his tongue against mine, and explored the softness of my waist and hips. My nipples hardened instantly as he caressed my body. I cried out, trailing a hand between us, capturing our combined essence, and bringing it to my mouth as his eyes darkened in lust.

"Playing with fire, Bria," Cairo stated, slamming into me.

"I like my odds, Cairo," I taunted. A frenzy of need and desire radiated through me at my statement. Cairo took that as a challenge and slid out of me, pushing my legs together, then driving inside at a fast pace. I whimpered in pleasure as his loud grunts and groans damn near drove me to a heart attack. I drenched his sheets as he circled his hips and pushed my legs against my chest. I couldn't move—I could only take the pleasure he was giving.

"I don't hear anything, Bria."

Shaking my head, I tried to push him away to no avail.

"Oh... ahhh... It's... Oh my God! Cairo." I panted as he buried his dick so deep, I felt him in my lungs.

"Told you, don't play with fire, baby." Cairo parted my lips with a kiss. The full story of how we came to be a couple weighed heavily on me. But like Amelia said, I was leading with my heart and not my head this time.

"What's wrong?" Cairo questioned, tracing my jaw.

"Nothing, give me a kiss," I said. To ease the tension, I practically jumped out of bed then grabbed my robe and headed to the kitchen to make lunch.

* * *

Amelia and Alana were meeting for the first time today at the photoshoot she had booked with her boss. I invited Amelia along to finally meet my best friend. I was already here because Cairo dropped me off. I looked at the door as Amelia ambled inside, and I jumped up to meet her.

"Hey, you made it," I said.

"I can't pass up getting the chance to hang with a world-renowned photographer, now can I?" she teased.

"Thanks for coming, it's my second time being out after the car wreck, and Cairo was pissed at first, but I convinced him to let up a little."

"Now I wonder how you made that happen," she joked and bumped her hip into me.

"You know us women have our ways. Anyway, I'm not staying long with King Cairo calling the shots."

"Does he know that's the nickname that you gave him?"

"No, and don't you tell him. I know he doesn't like me calling him Chase like the rest of you guys."

"Well, you're his woman, so he prefers Cairo, kind of the same as Aydin," Amelia said, sitting down on the couch behind the video monitor.

Alana walked over to us, and I tapped Amelia on the leg to get her attention.

"Amelia, this is Alana, my best friend." I introduced the two women and they shook hands.

"Nice to meet you, Amelia. You're married to Aydin, correct?" Alana asked.

"I am," she answered.

"How does it feel to be married to a sexy SEAL man?" Alana questioned.

I nudged Alana to cut out her questioning, sometimes she didn't know her audience and blurted out anything. She truly had no filter.

She motioned to her assistants and they brought over bottles of water. "Sorry, sometimes I can get carried away," Alana said.

Amelia blushed, scanning the studio. "No worries."

We thanked the assistants with a head nod.

"What are you shooting today, Alana?" I asked, changing the subject.

"It's mostly for editorial print, my boss is getting ready to update his website with new photos, so we pulled in a group of models."

"This is nice, and you're the assistant?" Amelia questioned.

"I am, and you work in your husband's company, right?" Alana replied with a hint of sarcasm.

Amelia took the bottle of water and gulped it down. "Office manager slash coordinator, some people find it boring, but I love it."

Alana's eyes roamed her face. "That's exciting. Well, I need to get back to work, ladies. It was nice meeting you, Amelia," Alana said, catching up with her boss as he called over for her.

"That was strange," Amelia remarked.

"What?"

Amelia frowned, tapped her finger on her cheek. "Your friend."

"What do you mean?" Alana had come across a little cold today, but I knew she was busy with work and might have gotten distracted. Hopefully they would have time in the future to connect.

"I can't put my finger on it but keep an eye on her."

Chapter Thirteen

Bria

A week had passed since I hung out with Alana and Amelia. Ever since Amelia made that statement, I had kept my distance. I couldn't bring myself to admit that I was probably jumping to conclusions and being irrational over nothing. Alana had been my best friend for over five years. Every accomplishment or issue I'd come across she'd been by my side. I couldn't see her ever hurting me. I looked up at the sound of the door opening as Cairo came in, dropped his keys on the table, and left his shoes at the door. It's something I'd started to do since staying at his place. I'd even picked up a lot of his habits and I found that strange.

I flipped through a magazine. "Long day?"

"Only because I was away from you," he said, bending down and kissing my cheek.

I peered up at him. "What happened today?"

"We had a conference call with the team in Memphis and talked about the logistics of the sentencing and your car wreck."

"You said Columbo investigated the phone records?"

"We expect them back tonight or tomorrow," Cairo said as he opened the fridge door and grabbed a bottle of water.

"What's it like going out on missions?" I inquired and put my feet into his lap so he could massage them.

He lingered on my left foot and ankle. "It takes mental agility, passion, strength, and a love for your country."

I tossed the magazine aside, leaned my head back, and relaxed from the feel of his hands. "King Cairo."

"What did you call me?" Cairo asked, turning toward me.

I grinned. "I called you King Cairo. It's a new nickname I made up."

He groaned, pulling me into his lap.

"How are you feeling? I mean, *really* feeling."

I turned my head and smiled. "I'm better, I promise. I have my days where I need to sit because I get tired faster, but overall I'm good."

"Once this is over, I want to take you out on the boat," Cairo said.

I tugged on his shirt. "Where's your boat?"

"In Nashville."

I smiled at the thought. "Any word on Albert?"

"Nothing concrete, Aydin is keeping me updated." The softness of his tone meant he was exhausted.

"Did you get an ID on the drivers? More than likely, they work for Moses."

"They do, but let's not talk about that. Let's discuss your parents at the hospital."

I rolled my eyes and moved back, but he stopped me. "Please don't bring that woman up."

"Has she called you lately?"

I waved off the question, since I knew how my mother operated. "Yeah, but I ignore her calls."

"I wish you could meet my parents. They'd probably want to adopt you," he joked.

"What were you like growing up?"

We interlocked our hands together. "The typical teenager, wanted to hang out with my friends and drive my dad's Mustang."

"My life was more structured with private school and no dating until I was eighteen, and even then, it was based on the guys she wanted me to date."

"Well, you're full-grown now in every way," he stated, kissing along my jawline toward the back of my neck.

"Aren't you tired of working?" I asked then moaned from his lingering kisses.

He smirked. "No."

"You're dangerous, King Cairo."

"As long as I'm only dangerous for you, baby."

Chapter Fourteen

Cairo

Pop! Pop!

I ducked as the shots flew past me. I investigated a warehouse that the Giovanni Cartel used for distribution, and we ended up catching a drug deal. I crouched down, checking the chamber of my gun as Aydin pointed for me to cover him. This wasn't supposed to end up like this. I had expected to have a typical day of checking on this lead from our meeting, but now I was in a deadly shootout.

"I got your back!" I shouted, leaning over and glancing to the side of the wall as two men returned fire. Soaquan and Maddux were on the opposite side shooting into a crowd of ten men compared to the four of us.

"Going in!" Aydin called out, jumping up and running to the side of the pole. I squeezed off three shots, and I heard one guy go down.

"Give it up and we'll let you live!" I shouted.

Pop! Pop!

"Fuck!" Another guy fell to the ground. Out the corner of my eye, I noticed that Aydin shot the taller one in the leg and he went down screaming. Aydin walked up on him and kicked his gun away.

Maddux and Soaquan finished off the last two of the ten as I continued to cover his back with my gun aimed at the suspect.

"Who do you work for?" Aydin asked.

"Fuck you!" he yelled, moaning as Aydin pushed the gun underneath his chin.

"The police are on their way, and you can either deal with them or us. I know they're probably sending word back to Moses about you giving him up," I said, manipulating him into giving up more evidence on the Giovanni Cartel. This crime family has been around for too long, and I was tired of seeing the killings running across my screen.

"All right, all right," he groaned.

"What was going down here?" I asked.

"Moses had a shipment of drugs coming in to take to jail."

How do you get them in jail without being noticed? I wondered.

"Man, I need a hospital," he said.

"You'll need a body bag if you don't answer our questions," Aydin said.

"Judge Bell helps us," he confessed.

We all stood stunned at his statement. To have a judge helping the dealer that he's presiding over would cause even more problems. The police and ambulance came in and started taking statements and cleaning up the bodies. I followed Aydin to the van.

"What are you thinking?" I asked.

"This won't be so simple for Bria," Aydin stated, opening the driver's door.

"This is more complicated than we thought."

"How are you two doing?"

"After the car wreck, we've been good. I've been a little overbearing, but she knows it's only because of the case right now."

"We've all been there with our women. It's surprising that it's you this time."

"What does that mean?"

"It means you were up there with Maddux as a ladies' man in the past, and over these past few weeks, you've changed your tune. You're not even bringing up retiring anymore," Aydin said.

"My plan is still to retire, I just need to get this case over with."

We made it back into the city, and Aydin dropped me off at my condo. He went to the office to complete the paperwork on the shooting today. I stepped on the elevator and a few minutes later it opened to my floor. I whistled as I made it to my door. Unlocking it, I heard soft music playing. The entire place was clean and smelled like lasagna.

"I wanted to surprise you with dinner," Bria said, wearing a short black cocktail dress. Her hair was pulled to the side in a low bun and her lips were coated with fiery red lipstick.

"What did I do to deserve this dinner?" I asked, removing my jacket and holster. I still had a little blood on me, so I stood back when she tried to hug me.

"What's wrong?" Bria asked.

"Let me shower first, I need to wash the day away."

I wanted to always be honest and let her know what to expect with the line of work I do.

"Ohhh."

"Give me ten minutes," I said, strolling to the bathroom.

* * *

I stalked to the living room dressed in a fresh shirt and jogging pants. Wrapping my arms around her waist as she continued cutting up tomatoes for a salad, I kissed the back of her neck.

"You smell ravenous."

She busted out in laughter. "Ravenous, Cairo?"

"Yep. Once dinner is over, I want dessert."

She tilted her head to the side. "I picked up your favorite ice cream."

"That's not the dessert I want. This right here is what I want," I announced, placing my hand between her legs. She leaned her head back on my shoulder. I continued kissing her and dipped my finger inside. It helped that she didn't wear any panties.

"Anything you want, let me finish getting dinner ready for you," Bria said, poking her lips out for a kiss.

"What did you do today?"

"Nothing. I tried to get caught up on some old cases, but I mostly watched TV."

"It won't be too much longer. Have faith in your man."

"I do. Can you grab the lasagna and follow me to the table?" Bria asked, lifting the bowl of salad and wine.

Grabbing the gloves, I picked up the lasagna and carried it over to the dining room table.

"I could get used to this," I said to her, pulling out her chair so she could sit.

Chapter Fifteen

Cairo

"Fuck... Bria!" I shouted, smacking the wall as I thrust into her from the behind. The anticipation for more launched through my body. I maneuvered her back against my chest, reaching around to the front and pinching her nipples. She grabbed my thigh digging her nails into my skin. A spine-tingling orgasm was slowly rising, and I watched as her chest rose and fell on ragged breaths.

"You understand, after this case, it's you and me," I told her, clutching her to me. I lifted one leg, clenched her waist, and settled into her slick folds. Her sucking matched my strokes, and I felt myself about to pass out three strokes along—that's how bad she had me gone in the head. I kissed her ear, whispering how good she felt and how much I loved her.

"Right there, baby. I love you, Cairo!" she yelled, almost falling over as my dick slid inside her pussy, my thumb grazing her nippple. The hunger inside grew even more as her toe-curling screams drowned out the sounds of our bodies slapping together.

"I'm about to come!" she shouted.

Before I could release, she dropped to her knees, my erection now throbbing in her hand. Her appetite for me was ravenous as she took me in her mouth. Bria watched as I moved her hair away from her face. I clenched the back of her neck, pumped in and out of her mouth. My hips rocked back and forth as my dick swelled. This primal ownership she had over my heart disoriented me and made me more aware of what I wanted out of life, and it was to be the man she needed.

"Bria, you're fucking killing me," I moaned out as she gently fondled my balls.

My dick betrayed me, unleashing inside her mouth as she sucked every drop down her throat.

"I like the way you wake me up, baby," I said, falling back on the bed as my breaths slowed to a calming pace.

Our hands interlocked as we peered up at the ceiling. I didn't know what was ahead for us, but I wanted to always remember this moment.

"Bria," I whispered, hearing her soft snores.

I laughed, knowing she always complained about me falling asleep first, and now it was her turn.

"I love you, baby."

* * *

The next day Aydin called a meeting with the team to go over the plan to catch Judge Bell and Albert. Bria was receiving death threats that Columbo looked into and found they originated from a burner phone. Maddux passed around a map of the courtroom as he talked about the day of the sentencing.

"Judge Bell doesn't suspect that we know he's taking a

payoff from Albert to give Moses a light term. We have to tread on thin ice to not ring the alarm." Maddux pointed to the map. Aydin watched with his hand on the right side of his jaw, listening intently.

"What are you thinking, Aydin?" I asked.

"We need backup. If I'm right about this, Moses will have people on the inside working with him to possibly kill Bria, even if his sentence is less."

Sighing, I leaned over the table, rubbing the top of my head.

"I think you're right, but Bria refuses to stay out of the courtroom the day of the sentencing."

"Victor said to use all of our resources so if we need the FBI to come instead of the local police, I suggest we put in a call now," Bishop suggested.

"Any more talks with the bartender, Soaquan?"

He grinned and rubbed his hands together.

"She was very forthcoming once we were away from the bar," Maddux answered.

My brow rose at his comment.

"Did you sleep with her?" He nodded, and we all groaned in annoyance.

"You're going to get tired of playing with these women," Bishop informed him. Scrolling through the documents, I noticed Judge Bell's name was on the search warrant for Moses' house and businesses. I wondered if Moses knew this and how he would feel if the Judge was setting him up.

"I got an idea," I announced, standing up and closing the file folder.

"What do you have?" Aydin questioned, walking alongside me toward the door of the office. Heading into the weapons room, I scanned my badge then walked inside with the team. The space was all black with cages that held guns and weapons. I picked up a vest and gun.

"Columbo told me that Judge Bell is looking to retire in the near future, as well as where the money came from for his wife's surgery."

"He's in deep?" Soaquan questioned, picking up the vest I passed him.

"Victor is on standby, what do you want me to say?" Bishop asked, holding up the phone. I nodded in answer.

Aydin took the call as my phone vibrated with a picture of Bria walking into the club that Moses owned.

"Shit!" I shouted as I slammed my hand on the wall. I tried to run out, but Soaquan stopped me, grabbing my arm. I shoved him off.

"She's in trouble!" I passed my phone over, and they all looked at each other. I knew that whatever happened needed to be a decision I could live with for the rest of my life. When I talked with her earlier, she didn't tell me she was going out today. I should have had Bishop stay with her.

"You have our support no matter what, Chase." Aydin gripped my shoulder, making eye contact with me.

"I can't let anything happen to her. Over these past few weeks, we've become close."

Each man held their hand out and we clasped them in solidarity before Aydin stated, "Brothers always."

We stalked out and piled into the truck. Soaquan drove toward the club as Aydin called and checked on Amelia.

"Babe, you good?" Aydin questioned.

"Hey, Aydin. What's wrong?" Amelia asked.

"We're going to get Bria," he answered, looking over at me in sadness.

"Oh, God! Do you need me to do anything?"

The car turned into traffic, then headed left to get on

the freeway. I tried calling Bria's cell but it went straight to voicemail, which meant something was wrong because she always picked up for me.

Aydin hung up with Amelia. "She said the last time she talked with Bria was two days ago."

"Columbo tracked her phone to a dumpster near the club," Maddux explained arriving at the location. It was the middle of the day, so the place wasn't too crowded, but several businesses in the area had a handful of cars out front. We checked our guns and tightened our bulletproof vests, pulled the blueprints, looking for the best way inside without getting Bria killed. My phone rang, and I picked it up without looking at the name.

"Is this Cairo Holden?" the voice asked.

"And this is...?" I motioned for them to track my call. Soaquan pulled up his phone and sent Columbo a message. Even with him living in Virginia, he could still follow anything on his computer.

"Mr. Holden, this is Moses Giovanni."

Cairo growled through the phone. "I know who you are."

"Then, you know the importance of my sentencing going off without a hitch."

"Where is she?" I demanded.

"She's safe for now."

"You won't get away with this. I can have you hurt in the jail cell," I said, hearing him chuckle on the other end of the call.

"She is a beautiful woman, I must say," Moses stated.

"I'm not the type of man you want to cross. If she's harmed in any way—"

"Now, Mr. Holden, or should I say Chase, I've learned a lot about you over the past few days. Don't let me being in jail confuse you into thinking that the people you love can't be touched," Moses said before hanging up.

"He's got her. Fuck!" I shouted, kicking the tire of the truck.

"Columbo said he can't guarantee she's inside. What do you want to do?" Soaquan inquired.

Pulling the gun out of my holster, I removed the safety, ready to take down anyone who'd hurt her. Holding my badge on the front of my vest, I gestured for Bishop and the backup team to take the back and sides of the building. Aydin was on my right when we busted inside, and everyone started scrambling and screaming in shock.

"Where is she?" I pointed the gun in the face of the bodyguard we blamed last time we met at the bar. He held up his hands in surrender, smirking. Not up for any games, I shot him in the foot and he fell down screaming.

"I won't ask again."

"Chase, back here!" Aydin yelled.

I motioned for Maddux to watch the door. I ran toward the hallway, down to the basement. Looking around, I saw money, guns, and drugs sitting on top of tables along with several naked, crying women.

"Where's Albert?" I questioned.

All three of them shook their heads, fear marring their faces.

"You're not in trouble. We're only looking for Albert. My men will help you get out of this and find a better job instead of doing this for money," Aydin told the trio of women.

The girl wearing her hair up in a ponytail raised her hand. I gestured for her to speak.

"He rushed out of here about twenty minutes ago. He didn't say where he was going though," she responded.

"Was anyone with him?" I questioned.

"No, he was alone," she answered.

"He didn't get far, Chase. Let's get out of here and let the police figure this out," Soaquan replied. We walked out of the room and bumped into the police. Maddux must have informed them of what was taking place because they were arresting everyone, including the waitresses. Pushing the door open, I looked around the area, wondering where Albert would take Bria.

"I don't think she's with him, it was too easy for us," Maddux remarked, and I nodded, feeling the same way. Moses was playing games and taunting me.

"Call the Commander and see if he can get a warrant to the judge's home," I muttered, opening the truck door and jumping in on the driver's side.

Buckling my seatbelt, I made a U-turn in the middle of the street and pushed the gas to its fullest speed to get across town quickly. Based on Moses' conversation, I felt he pushed the judge to get involved beyond his regular sentencing duties.

Chapter Sixteen

Cairo

"I wonder if the judge's wife is really having surgery. It all seems convenient when you think about it," Bishop stated.

"My gut is telling me the same thing." I blew out a breath in frustration.

The phone vibrated, and a text came through. I brought it up and saw a photo of Bria in a room wearing the same clothes from earlier today.

"Call for backup now. I swear if anything happens to her, I'm burning this place down."

I parked in front of the judge's house and jumped out. Abe took the keys out of the ignition as I started stomping toward the front door.

Aydin pulled me back to slow me down. "Wait, calm down, Cairo. We need to think about this. It's a judge's house."

I was fuming, ready to shoot up the entire place, not caring who was inside.

"She's there. I'm telling you, Aydin." I paced back and forth.

"I know but slow down and get your head right."

"What if it was Amelia? Huh?"

"I hear you and I've been on the receiving end of being ready to turn the world upside down for the one you love, but you need to think straight right now," Aydin answered.

I complied, banging on the door lightly until the lock turned and Judge Bell stood in front of us. I reached out and gripped his neck, pushing him against the wall.

"The minute I think you're lying, say goodbye to your family because I have nothing to lose," I spat harshly.

"Get off my property before I call the police," Judge Bell yelled.

"Wrong answer," I said, slinging him on the ground then running into his house, calling her name.

"Soaquan, put him in handcuffs until we get back," I overheard Aydin say.

After I searched the kitchen, I opened the door next to the kitchen and saw it was an empty bathroom. Turning, I crossed the archway, kicking in the master bedroom door. Opening the closet doors, I was getting pissed even more.

"Fuck!" I shouted.

Soaquan walked Judge Bell over, pushing him down on the chair. I pulled up the image on my phone, showing him that we knew he received money from Moses and it was deposited in an offshore account.

"Did your wife really have surgery?" I interrogated, shoving the phone in his face. He grimaced as he gazed at the screen.

"How much is Moses paying you to betray your oath as a judge?"

He still didn't answer.

I shrugged, passing my phone to Aydin, and punched Judge Bell in the face.

"Ah!" Judge Bell cried, falling to the floor.

"Answer my question!"

Through slow breaths, I helped him sit up, tapping him gently across the face. "Focus. How much did he pay you, and where is Bria?" I demanded.

"Two million to keep his operation going while he's in jail and let him out in three to five on good behavior," he muttered.

"Too bad you won't get to see any of that money."

"She's down in the basement," Judge Bell stated.

"Where's your wife?" I asked.

"Staying with family. After Albert came to my house threatening me, I sent her away."

My eyes rose in shock, and I took off to find the basement. It was the last door at the end of the house that no one noticed. It looked like a regular closet but when I turned on the light and pushed the side panel it opened, and stairs took me into the basement. Bria was standing in the corner with a knife ready to fight back. She dropped the knife and ran into my arms. Hearing her tears broke me because I didn't protect her as I should have.

"You're safe, shush... you're safe now." I rubbed her back, trying to calm her down.

"Cairo, I thought he was going to kill me." Bria whimpered, clinging to my chest.

The rest of the team searched as I walked Bria upstairs, sitting on the couch as the FBI came in and out.

"Sit here, tell me what happened," I commanded her, not leaving her side.

"I went to the coffee shop around the corner from your condo. I didn't think anything could happen, and before I got there, I was snatched, and something covering my face made me black out."

"Do you know how many men there were?" Aydin inquired.

Her tears were still falling down her face and she leaned on my shoulder. I wrapped an arm around her, pulling her in close. Maddux and Bishop stood around us, looking just as angry as me.

"Two, I think. I don't remember it happened so fast," Bria answered.

"Did they touch you?" I asked hesitantly.

She shook her head. "No, they just threw me in the basement. I can't believe the judge is in on all of this."

"Come on, let's get you home. I didn't think you'd want me calling your parents."

"I'll call my dad, but I doubt my mom even cares."

Bria stood, and I helped her leave the house as the FBI escorted Judge Bell out in front of us. He stopped and turned toward her.

"Bria, I hope one day you can forgive me. It wasn't supposed to get this far," Judge Bell said.

Slap! Slap!

Bria hit the judge across his face twice and it took Aydin and me to pull them apart.

"It's over, baby, don't worry about him anymore."

"What about Moses?" Bria questioned.

"He's still locked up, and the sentencing is coming up soon. We'll get someone to replace you Bria," I told her, and she jerked out of my hold.

"I'm going to the sentencing, Cairo. He won't win." Bria walked away from me. I reached for her, but she held up her hand for me to stop.

"Bria..."

"No, I've worked too hard not to finish this and I refuse to let him win," she responded, opening the passenger door, jumping in, and slamming it shut. I sighed and ran a hand down my face, thinking of how to get her to see it wasn't a good idea to force herself to the sentencing and being in the same room with them right now.

I walked around and hopped in on the driver's side as Aydin finished talking with our point of contact in the FBI as they started walking out with boxes of documents. I placed my hand on her thigh and squeezed it gently, letting her turn to me.

"I understand you want to see this case to the finish line, and I just want you to give yourself a few days to rest," I explained, putting the key in the ignition.

The back door opened, Aydin and Maddux put their seatbelts on then I drove toward home.

* * *

An hour later Bria came out of the shower with a towel secured around her. It was going on seven at night and food had been delivered, so she didn't have to figure out what to eat. I patted the space next to me on the bed for her to sit down. She came in close, and I wrapped my arms around her waist, taking in the fresh coconut smell of her body wash.

"What are you thinking?" she asked.

"I think you're putting too much pressure on yourself with this case."

"You're right, I am, but I fought to get this case. Partially to prove to myself I can win. But also to show my mom that I can do the work and don't need her to dictate my life."

"Are you hungry?"

"A little."

"Get dressed and come to the kitchen so you can eat, and we can continue our conversation."

"Mhm... Okay." She leaned over, pecking my lips. I slid my tongue into her mouth, wanting more but it was too early for sex. I stood up, kissed her palm, and walked out of the bedroom so she could finish getting dressed in her pajamas.

I had food from the local Vietnamese restaurant laid out on plates, and her favorite snacks stocked if she needed them. Bria came around the corner wearing black tights and one of my white T-shirts.

"I thought you were going to put on your pajamas."

Scratching her nose, she replied, "I wanted something different tonight. You don't mind, do you?"

"I prefer you in whatever makes you comfortable, baby," I said, kissing her forehead.

"Good, so I wanted to get started on the files that the FBI took from Judge Bell's house. Potentially there could be more corruption that he's part of that I could bring to the mayor and governor."

"Do you believe the mayor can be trusted? I mean, we know some police are on Moses' payroll, and now Judge Bell, so it wouldn't be too farfetched if the mayor was involved," I stated.

Bria put a fork full of her noodles in her mouth, washing it down with water.

"Probably not, but I can try to see what the DA says, and if they try to bury what I find, then we'll do it your way."

"My way is you recuse yourself from this case," I replied.

"If I leave this case, it'll be another case that comes

along with a dangerous criminal. I love my job, Cairo, same as you love being a SEAL."

I agreed in theory, so I smiled at her and lifted her chin for a kiss.

"Finish eating so we can start looking through some of the files."

"You had them bring everything here?"

"Not everything because the FBI is doing an investigation. But Victor had a little pull and helped me out."

I strolled into the living room and grabbed two boxes off the floor and removed the tops, picking up several files before laying everything on the coffee table.

Bria walked over with both our plates and sat next to me on the couch and we read over testimony from some of the witnesses in the case. For the rest of the evening, we laid out photos and names of businesses that Moses was stealing from to keep his fear tactics in place.

Four hours later, I was awakened by my phone vibrating. Bria started to wake, and I rubbed her thigh underneath the covers, keeping her back to my chest for comfort.

Aydin: You good?

Me: Barely, she had a nightmare.

Aydin: Let me know what we can do.

Me: Find Albert for me.

Aydin: Columbo is running his face against computer databases, we'll catch him soon.

Me: Thanks, Aydin.

Chapter Seventeen

Bria

It was the day of the sentencing. All of my hard work was coming together as we waited for Judge Thompson to come out of her chambers. Feeling eyes on me, I looked to my left. Moses glared at me, a huge bruise on his face. I heard from Cairo that he was in a fight, but he didn't give me all the details. I wondered if he had something to do with it because ever since I was kidnapped, he'd been by my side, not even letting me leave alone to go to the mailroom in his building. It surprised me that I was still staying at his place every night, but it was time for me to go home and figure out my next moves after this case. I mean, he only came into my life to protect me, I couldn't expect him to give up everything to be with me in New York. The judge entered the courtroom, and everyone stood at the bailiff's command. I looked behind me at the SEAL team was sitting there, prepared to escort Moses back to California.

"You may take a seat," Judge Thompson said. The DA listened to my concerns about Judge Bell and Moses, plus Albert had confessed about the judge taking a bribe. They gave him a lenient jail sentence of five to ten years after he turned over everything on Moses and the hit that was put out against me. At first, I wanted to demand a longer jail sentence, but Cairo was right in that I needed to move on and focus on the bigger prize, and that was putting Moses away for a very long time. The reporters in the back continued taking photos and recording Moses as he whispered in his attorney's ear. No amount of negotiation would keep him from the crimes he committed throughout the city.

"Mr. Giovanni, after reading all the witness statements and reading over your file, I've made my final decision. You may stand."

He and Sean stood up together.

"You are hereby sentenced to twenty years to run concurrently with ten years for the attempted assassination of Prosecutor Bria Dawson," Judge Thompson announced, and the entire room gasped in shock.

"Your Honor!" Sean shouted as the police handcuffed Moses.

"Thank you, jury, for your service today. This court is adjourned," Judge Thompson said, banging her gavel. I let out a long-held breath as reporters clamored around me to get a statement. I wasn't looking to become a famous attorney from this case. It was about seeing justice prevail and putting a criminal behind bars. I closed my briefcase, looked up, and caught Moses winking at me as he was hauled off. Cairo and his team followed behind, and I was sure I wouldn't hear from him for the next few hours. I planned on going home and opening a bottle of wine to celebrate that this was all over.

"Miss Dawson, is this the outcome you wanted?" a reporter asked, pushing the mic in front of my face.

"The outcome of a criminal being punished for his crimes? Yes, I'm thankful to the judge and the jury for their hard work," I replied.

"What about your relationship with Cairo Holden?"

"If you want to continue this conversation about Moses Giovanni, we can," I told him.

"The reports are coming out that you made a deal for Albert to get less time if he flipped on Moses. Any truth to that?"

"The prosecutor's job is to look at all evidence, I did my job, and the judge and jury decided what Albert's sentence was going to be. I can't speak for them."

"Do you think the Giovanni Cartel will continue in their absence?" the reporter asked.

"The FBI and local authorities are monitoring them and keeping the DA updated. Thank you, gentlemen, I have to go."

* * *

I was back in my house with the TV on, watching the entire case up to the sentencing. Cairo hadn't called me back. Surprisingly my mom called, but I let it go to voicemail. I wasn't prepared to fight with her after the day I'd had. Putting everything back in order after the break-in and maybe taking a vacation was on my list because the last eight months had become a rollercoaster of life and death. My phone rang again, and I picked it up to have a long-overdue conversation with my mom.

"Hello," I said.

"Are you avoiding me, Bria?" Mom asked.

"Yes," I answered.

"Why is it so bad to want what's best for your child? You can't be happy with that man."

"My relationship with Cairo is none of your business," I snapped, taking another sip of the red wine I opened when I came home.

"You're really a foolish little girl. He can't provide for you the way Kory could have."

"Tell the truth, this is about you and your overbearing stronghold to make me the perfect daughter in your eyes. Which is something I could never be, and I'm done giving you that power," I spat.

"Don't you dare raise your voice at me!" she yelled, and I hung up, blocking her number for the rest of the night. If it was an emergency, I knew my father would call me. Standing up, I started to go take a shower when I heard a knock at my door. Bypassing my bathroom, I grabbed the baseball bat and peeked through the window to see who was at my door this late.

"Hey," I said, opening the door and letting Cairo walk inside.

He kissed me on the cheek and removed his holster and gun.

"Hungry?" I asked, ready to go into the kitchen and fix him a plate. He stopped me from leaving, grabbing my elbow and pulling me into his arms, giving me a searing kiss on the lips.

Chapter Eighteen

Cairo

"What was that for?" she asked.

"For just being you and looking sexy as hell in court today."

"It felt good to see that smirk fall off his face when the judge said twenty to thirty years."

"Yeah, I have the pleasure of flying him to Nashville tomorrow with the guys, then Memphis."

"I forgot about you having to go back home so soon," she muttered, tightening her arms around my waist and burying her face in my chest. I ran a hand up and down her back, soothingly.

"You can come with me."

She froze at my statement. "What?"

"To Nashville, come down there and see if you like it, maybe even move," I suggested.

"I can't."

"Why not?"

"I want to do things on my terms, and I'm not saying you're pushing me at all, but between my mom, Kory trying to push his way back in, and us getting together so fast, I don't think it's a good idea to up and move."

"How did your ex get in this conversation?" I questioned, stepping back, putting distance between us, and sliding my hands in my pockets.

"Cairo, today was a major win for me. Can we talk about something else, please?"

"Sure, Bria."

"What time are you leaving tomorrow?" she asked, going to the kitchen. I went along with the change of conversation for now until I completed the mission tomorrow.

"I need to be up at six, and our flight leaves at eight," I answered, grabbing the plate of spaghetti and salad.

"Are the guys excited to get back home?"

"Yeah."

"Did you talk with your parents?"

"Yes."

"Cairo, is this how it's going to be for the rest of the night? These one-word answers?" she snapped, throwing her hands on her hips.

"Probably."

"You're childish," she said, tossed the paper towel on the counter, and walked off. I was too heated to follow her because I knew my temper and blowing up wouldn't solve the problem. We did move fast under abnormal circumstances, but my love for her wasn't based on me keeping her safe. Trying to run her life like her parents or her ex wasn't even in my DNA.

Sighing, I dropped the fork, not finishing my dinner, and went to find her in her bedroom. I hadn't even brought up her coming back to her place instead of mine after the trial.

I stood in the doorway, watching her switch between TV channels as she laid against the headboard.

"I apologize if I hurt your feelings," I said, coming in and closing the bedroom door.

"Thank you," she muttered, not taking her eyes off the TV.

"Can I sit here?" I pointed to the edge of the bed where her feet were.

She nodded, and I lifted her legs, placing them in my lap.

"What do you need?" I questioned.

"I need you to give me some time. I love you, Cairo, deeply, and I don't want to end what we have. I just need to be me for a little while."

"And that means we'll try long distance?"

Bria fidgeted with her hands as she peered at me. "I know you don't want to, and I understand if you want to see other women."

"That's never even been on my radar, Bria."

She bit her lip. "Okay, sorry I mentioned it."

"Can I have a kiss now?"

"You can have more than kisses. How about I send you off on your trip with the best blow job of your life?" she teased, sliding her legs from my lap, then getting down on the floor in front of me. I removed my vest and shirt, helping her unbuckle my pants. Falling back on the bed, my eyes fluttered closed with her warm lips wrapped around my dick.

* * *

The airport wasn't too crowded as we walked inside with a police escort. The minute my alarm went off, I jumped up, showered, and dressed in the same clothes I came to her house in. Aydin was ready to get back home, as he'd already sent Amelia back a few days ago. All the guys wondered if Bria would move to Nashville, and I told them not at the moment. We'd try flying back and forth until we decided where our relationship would go. Since Moses was high risk, we had the flight to ourselves with US Marshals on board to help transport him. He wasn't smiling like he had in the courtroom, and I knew it was because the charges he had pending in Memphis would stack another ten to twenty years on his New York sentence from the gang killings. I didn't get a chance to say goodbye to Bria because I didn't want to wake her after our long night of lovemaking. If that was my last time seeing her, I wanted to have a memory.

"You sure you're up for this?" Aydin questioned, sitting down across from me on the plane.

We put Moses in the middle aisle surrounded by all four of us and the marshals. He was handcuffed with no place to go. The stewardess would have to feed him if he got hungry.

"I am."

"Women have a way of making you question everything about yourself," Aydin said.

"That's true and they drive you crazy," I joked.

"Amelia hopes she'll change her mind."

"Do you think I gave up too quickly?"

"I can't say. Every situation is different."

"We all saw you go after Amelia, and she eventually settled with you."

"Yeah, but Amelia is different, and she wasn't dealing with distance between us," Aydin stated.

"Maybe space will help us both figure out what we

want. Eventually, she will need to decide where her heart belongs."

The pilot announced that we were preparing for landing and to buckle our seatbelts. I laid my head back and looked up at the ceiling, picturing Bria and I naked in bed, confessing our love for each other.

After we landed and loaded up the van, we drove to the courthouse and signed in Moses, handing off his case files to the local prosecutor and DA. We didn't have too long of a drive to our respective homes, so we stopped off at the local bar. Opening the door, I saw Nicco, Faulkner, and Jasper already at a table with drinks. I waved the bartender over and ordered a scotch since Aydin was the designated driver today.

"To another successful mission, fellas," Nicco announced, holding his drink in the air.

"We saw you guys on the news, and Columbo told us about you dating the prosecutor?" Faulkner questioned.

I scratched my beard, not knowing how much I wanted to talk about the situation and not look like a lovesick teenager.

"It's a work in progress at the moment," I replied, taking a sip of my drink.

"That sounds like you're in love," Maddux teased, and I flipped him off. All of the guys laughed, slapping me on the shoulder.

"You'll end up like our fearless leader and married in no time. Don't stress yourself out," Nicco told me with a smirk on his face.

Am I ready for marriage? We'd never talked about a ring, I thought. To distract myself, I listened to Maddux tell us another story about one of his many dates as we all hung out for the rest of the night. I swallowed the rest of the scotch and left a fifty on the table for the waitress.

"Are you ready to head out?"

"I need to stop and grab something on the way home."

"What do you need to get?"

"Something that will hopefully let me know if I'm doing the right thing."

Chapter Nineteen

Cairo

Two weeks later

"I can tell something's not right with my son," my mom said, handing me a glass of tea. I liked to come out to the backyard and watch the lake and gather my thoughts.

"Dad send you out here?" I quizzed.

"No, my own motherly instincts."

Grinning, I kissed her cheek.

"So, tell me why you're looking miserable."

"I miss her."

"Then why are you here and not New York?"

"We live in two different states, it wouldn't work, and honestly, she doesn't want to be tied down with a husband and kids."

"Did she say that to you?" Mom asked.

"Not in those exact words."

"Communication is critical. Cairo, look at your father and me. We've been married for over forty years, and I recognize when something is wrong by looking at him."

"Did you ever feel stuck when you got pregnant with

me? Like you felt your life was over once the baby came along?"

"Yes, for a little while. Is that the problem with Bria?"

"Her parents, well, her mom basically ran her entire life, and she's always trying to decide things for her. She even tried to fix her up with her ex."

"Let me guess, she refused and thought you would potentially end up like her mom and put demands on her life," Mom exclaimed. And I nodded in answer.

"It sums up our relationship and don't forget the part about us only getting together because her life was in danger," I replied.

"I constantly tell you to fight for what you love. Bria sounds like a headstrong girl, and I'd love to meet her one day. The only opinions that matter are hers and yours."

"So, if I go out and elope tomorrow, you won't have an issue with that?" I teased.

"Now you're talking crazy, boy. I'll leave you alone to figure out your thoughts, and lunch will be ready soon," Mom stated, swiveled around, and strolled into the house.

* * *

After we had lunch and I helped my mom around the house, I finally made it to my house, which was two blocks from theirs. I pulled into my driveway and noticed a car parked out front. Grabbing my gun, I took off the safety, prepared to handle whoever decided to trespass on my property. They locked up Moses, but we still had our ears to the streets in case he sent anyone to Bria's or my house. Even though we hadn't talked, I still made sure she was safe. The door opened, and Bria stepped out carrying a bag. Relaxing, I put the safety back on and put the gun away.

Watching her walk toward me, I wanted to run and pick her up in my arms and never let her go; another part wanted to ignore her the same way she ignored me for the last two weeks and didn't take my calls.

"Hey."

"What are you doing here, Bria?"

"Hopefully, making the right decision."

"Whose car are you in?"

"It's a rental."

"I see one bag, how long are you planning to stay?"

"Can we go inside?" she asked.

"Depends on the answer to my next question."

"What's your question, Chase?" she asked.

I wanted to take her over my knee for making me agonize over her all this time.

"Are you here for good or visiting?"

"I'm wherever you are," she declared, dropping the bag on the ground before she stepped up, closing the gap between us and grasping my chin. I met her halfway as our lips collided in haste and desperation. I'd never wanted to be inside of her so badly, it was like my life depended on it. The distance was torture, not seeing her every day or holding her in my arms as we slept after making love. I missed being able to talk about our days and hearing her laugh and seeing her sexy smile. I lifted her bridal style. Walking up to my steps, I forgot to get my keys out, so I maneuvered her to grab them out of my pocket. Pushing open the door, I started to move to my bedroom before she called out for me to stop.

"We can't leave my bag, Cairo."

"We'll get it later."

"Are you that horny? That you can't wait two seconds for me to pick up my bag?" she joked, and I shrugged in answer, continuing to walk to my bedroom. Living in Hendersonville, I had eight thousand square feet of land in a modest two-story home with five bedrooms and three baths. I hoped she was ready for babies because I planned on making up for the lost time. Placing her on top of the bed, we ripped each other's clothes off, not waiting another second. I sucked her bottom lip as she caressed my back. Falling in between her legs, I wanted to savor every moment getting reacquainted with her body. I figured after a few rounds she'd let me enjoy feasting on her sweet lips. Lining my dick up, I eased in her warm pussy, almost ready to burst, and I had to pull back because otherwise, I would come too quickly.

"I missed you..." she moaned out, reaching for me to come closer. I bent down and kissed her, letting her wrap her arms around my neck and her leg over my thigh.

"Baby, I missed you too. Never leave me again."

"I won't," she cried out when I slid out and pushed back in.

"Promise me," I pressed, picking up the pace.

"I... I...Promise!"

"I can't hear you," I demanded, circling my hips and hitting her G-spot, watching her eyes roll in the back of her head.

"Cairo... I sorry... Ughhh ... God!"

"Ahhh... Fuck, I love you, Bria," I shouted, pulling out of her, falling to my back, and helping her straddle me.

"Come ride your man," I said.

"I missed us," she whimpered as she lowered herself onto my swollen length.

"Stop letting the outside noise get in your head. It's you and me that matters."

"Me and you," she repeated, arched forward, smashed her lips on mine.

We spent the next few hours reuniting in the bed and shower, then talking about the past two weeks and what she'd been up to. She wore one of my T-shirts, and I had on pajama bottoms and no shirt.

"I pretty much asked for a transfer out here, and I talked with Amelia and Aydin about some places for rent."

"You're staying with me, and that's final."

"Are you sure?"

"Yes, the last thing we need is more distance between us when you live in the same state."

"Okay."

"What about your parents? How did they take it?"

"My dad was okay with me moving, but my mom was still pissed and said if I moved, I could kiss my inheritance goodbye."

"You have your own money. Baby, I hate to tell you this, but your mom is over the top crazy."

"I know, and you'd think at thirty-three she'd cut the cord, but nope. So, I decided to cut her off."

"How do you feel about that? It's your mom, babe."

"Took some time and after talking with Alana, I figured the best thing was to keep her negative energy away from me. I'm doing well in life, and she can call me a disappointment if she wants."

"Never think you're less than because you're not. You're a queen in my eyes," I said, and she grinned.

"When do I get to meet your parents?"

"We can meet them tomorrow. Right now, I want you all to myself for the next few hours to make up for you not calling me during the past two weeks." I lifted her chin to stare into her eyes.

"I didn't mean to ignore you. I was just busy getting things prepared for transferring out here and then getting my place put on the market. I thought once I got here, we could talk in person."

"Talking will happen, but right now, I need you on your knees with your ass in the air," I demanded, picking up an old tie to have a little fun. She got down on her knees, and I came behind her and used the scarf to cover her eyes. I planned to pleasure her with my tongue and dick until we both passed out.

Chapter Twenty

Bria

The next day Amelia and I were talking on FaceTime after we'd had lunch earlier. She was telling me about the latest work she was doing at the office.

"Aydin wants me to take a vacation."

"That would be nice, a little R&R. You two deserve that after everything you've been through together," I answered.

Looking in my closet, I pulled out a gold and white strapless dress for my date tonight with Cairo. During lunch, he texted about having dinner with his parents, and I finished catching up on some of my work early, so I was excited to finally meet them. He told me they were the complete opposite of my parents, so hopefully, they liked me.

"What do you think?"

She stared at me. "That's cute. Have you heard from Alana?" Amelia asked.

"No, my schedule has been crazy lately, so I haven't talked with her, why?"

"Curious if she's reached out to you since you moved."

"No. Cairo thinks to give it time, our schedules are so busy. When you've been friends with someone for so long we get caught up in daily lives."

"I understand, but you two haven't talked in a few months and she's traveling," she replied.

"She's probably somewhere with a new man." I chuckled.

I tossed the dress on the bed and switched the phone to stand on the charger so I could change my clothes. I came to stand back in front of her with the dress and posed.

"What do you think?"

"Sexy lady."

I laughed picking up the phone. "Once I get back, I'll call you back," I said.

"Have fun."

I nodded hanging up with her as the front door opened and closed. I fluffed out my hair and looked in the mirror, putting a little lipstick on my lips and sliding my feet in the black heels.

"It's nice walking in and finding you here," Cairo said, stood at the corner.

I twirled in front of him. "Get used to it because it's real."

"Are you ready?"

I ambled over to the dresser. "Yep, let me grab my purse."

"Cool. My parents are out front."

I paused. "What!"

He reached to grab my hand. "Calm down, you'll be fine."

"I thought we were meeting them at their place or something."

"I wanted you to be comfortable, and bringing them here was the best decision."

"How do I look?"

"Beautiful as usual. Come on, let's go." He extended his hand, and I grasped his palm, letting him lead me out of the bedroom. We walked down the hallway, turning the corner, and I noticed his parents and my dad. I lifted my hand to my face, trying to stop myself from crying.

"What are you doing here?" I questioned my dad.

He reached out for me, and I ran to his arms, crying.

"I'm sorry, baby. For everything."

"Where's Mom?" I quietly asked.

"I left her, sweet pea."

I jerked back in shock. "Why?"

"I wasn't happy, and I was tired of living a lie, and you need to do the same," he said.

Cairo pulled me to his side and introduced me to his parents. "Bria, I'd like you to meet my mom and dad."

I shook their hands, and his mom gave me a hug.

"You're so beautiful, Bria," his mom said.

"Thank you, ma'am."

"Girl, call me mom."

I looked to Cairo, and he winked at me, dropped to his knee, and slid a small black box out of his pocket.

"Cairo—"

"I want you to know you can always count on me to be the one there when you're feeling sad, happy, excited. Finding your passion for life as I continue down my path of being a SEAL."

"You're not retiring?" I asked, and everyone chuckled.

"Bria Dawson, will you marry me?" he asked, opening the box to show off a gorgeous one-carat diamond heart-shaped ring.

"Yes!" I shouted, my hand now shaking from him placing the ring on my finger. He stood up, pulling me into his chest, grabbed both sides of my face, and kissed me, shoving his tongue into my mouth as our parents clapped and cheered.

Epilogue

Cairo

A year later, we were married, sailing around Greece with our family and friends. I thought back to our wedding and how beautiful she looked that day and the overwhelming need I felt to keep her safe at all times. I vowed to always be there for her, and now I had the privilege of keeping them all safe. Seeing Bria in the two-piece bathing suit underneath the wrap dress taking photos with Amelia made me smile. I felt a tap on my shoulder, and Aydin crossed his arms, watching the girls laugh and joke around.

"It's a beautiful sight to see," Aydin said, and I nodded.

"Yeah."

"Can you believe you were about to retire that day we were at the courthouse? You nearly passed up on meeting your future wife."

I groaned. "Don't remind me about that day. Dealing with Moses and the cartel was exhausting."

"Well, now you have a wife and one day, you'll be a father. Are you still retiring?"

"I'm debating, man. She's taking some time off before

she goes back to being a prosecutor and we're talking about having kids."

"How do you feel about that? I mean, her job is dangerous," Aydin asked.

"That's what I'm afraid of, and she's still young. You know I was hesitant to get involved with a woman. Bria's worth the work."

"You know I support you no matter what your decision is if you fully retire," Aydin stated.

Bria slid beside me, wrapping her arms around my waist and kissing me on the cheek.

"Having fun?" I asked, squeezing her waist.

Bria grinned. "Yeah, babe. Are you happy?"

"More than happy but ready for everyone to get off the boat so I can have you to myself."

Amelia walked over, standing next to Aydin.

"I'm so happy for you both. I wish you didn't have to go through so much last year to be together. Brings back how we met, Aydin," Amelia said.

"Any word from the Giovanni Cartel after Moses' death?" Bria asked.

"Nothing for you to worry about," I told her, not wanting to change the positive energy of our trip. Aydin and I made eye contact in confirmation that the latest information we received showed that the Cartel was brewing in New York again, and the team might go out to investigate. He wanted me to go with them. Leaving Bria right after getting married and working on having a baby would be wrong. But I'd do anything to keep her safe.

"I'm ready to test out the bed in the back," Bria whispered in my ear, running a hand up to my chest. I lifted her hand, kissing her palm.

"You're torturing me in this outfit." I groped her ass in front of our friends, not caring.

"That's the sign for us to leave you two alone. Come on, Amelia, let the newlyweds have their moment," Aydin said, walking off as Amelia giggled behind him. I chuckled, kissing Bria on the lips.

"Mmmm...Thank you, baby."

Pecking her lips again, I lifted my head and asked, "What are you thanking me for?"

"For protecting me, not only from the Cartel but protecting my heart as well."

"Always," I responded, pulling her close to my chest.

* * *

I hope you enjoyed Bria and Cairo's story. Also, check out the next book in the series, "**Consume Me**," a best friend's brother's romance coming up next.

Have you checked out "**His Peace Her Pleasure?**" Click here https://books2read.com/u/3JJroP a billionaire, steamy romance.

Also, steamy romance that includes bodyguard tropes, one-night stands, marriage troubles, and more here "*Seeking In Romance 1-6*" https://books2read.com/u/4ELGLe

Don't forget if you love Fling romances, bodyguard, and forced proximity, then check out "**Protecting Chanel**" https://books2read.com/u/mqwPB8

If you love brother's best friend romance, you'll love "**Sensual**" **here** https://books2read.com/u/49lYYM with a dash of steamy romance.

Check out Bodyguard Romance, military, romantic

suspense here ***"Protecting Bria"*** https://books2read.-com/u/bQJkjd_

Follow college romance and more characters in ***"Taste"*** here https://books2read.com/u/bpz1Ng

How about a steamy, medical romance? Check out ***"Haven"*** https://books2read.com/u/4jAvyZ a steamy, enemies-to-lovers romance.

Please also check out my ***"Love Don't Live Here Anymore Vanessa Andrew"*** https://books2read.-com/u/mBOWGZ a steamy curvy girl, enemies-to-lovers romance.

Follow that up with a workplace vacation romance in **"Love Don't Live Here Anymore Isabella Andrew"** https://books2read.com/u/brVNO7

More workplace, boss romances with **"Love by Design Box Set 1-3"** https://books2read.com/u/m2ldEk

Reader Questions

1. Do you think Bria and Cario belong together?

2. Would you like to see one of his friends get a HEA?

3. What do you think of Bria's parents?

4. What do you think of her best friend?

5. Should Cario retire?

Playlist: Protecting Bria

1. Rihanna-Love on The Brain

2. Patti LaBelle-If Only You Knew

3. Sadie-No Ordinary Love

4. Alicia Keys-No One

5. Michael Jackson-The Way You Make Me Feel

6. Miguel-Adorn

7. BabyFace-When Can I See You Again

Sneak Peek

Tempt Me: Billionare Boy's Club Book 4

Can Bia finally get over her crush for her brother's best friend turned billionaire businessman?

Kofi stole Bia's heart a long time ago. She's made a habit of ignoring her body whenever he was around. He's a playboy, a billionaire, and completely off limits and now he's her biggest business rival.

Bia's always been his best-friend's little sister, that's why Kofi didn't feel threatened at all when he learned that he and Bia were going to be working together. Besides, he's always waited for the right opportunity to ask her about a text she sent him one drunken night, it's time for her to explain herself.

Stepping into Kofi's world is harder than Bia imagined. Not only is he respected and experienced in his field, but he's also cocky and more handsome than ever before.

Will Kofi get the answers he's looking for, or will Bia bow out before things get too heated in the boardroom?

Catalog of Releases By Keke Renée

•Wet Heat (Wet Heat Series Book 1)

•Every time We Touch Novelette (Wet Heat Book 2 Series)

•His Peace, Her Pleasure

•Baby, It's Cold Outside

•Love Don't Live Here Anymore, Vanessa Andrew Book 1

•Love Don't Live Here Anymore, Isabella Andrew Book 2

•One Night Only-A Novelette (Love By Design Book 1)

•Cassian and Savannah (Love By Design Book 2)

•Deidra's Love (Love By Design Book 3)

•Protecting Bria TN Seal Security Nashville Division Book 1

•Protecting Chanel TN Seal Security Nashville Division Book 2

•Protecting Yanira TN Seal Security Nashville Division Book 3

•Haven

•Taste (A New Adult romance)
•Sensual
•Seek To Please
•Seek To Bare
•Seek To Touch
•Seek To Love
•Seek To Trust
•Seek To Earn

Thank you so much for reading and if you enjoyed the crazy ride and decide to leave a review we'd truly appreciate the support.

Catalog of Releases By Chiquita Dennie

Series

Struck in Love

The Early Years-A Prequel Short Story

Ruthless:Antonio and Sabrina Book 1

Savage: Antonio and Sabrina Book 2

Beast: Antonio and Sabrina Book 3

Captivated By His Love:Janice and Carlo

Brutal: Antonio and Sabrina Booke 4

Redemption: Antonio and Sabrina Book 5

Heart of Stone

Broken, Book 1 (Emery & Jackson)

A Valentine's Day Short Book 1.5 Emery & Jackson

Rebirth, Book 2 (Jordan and Damon)

Reveal, Book 3 (Angela and Brent)

Bottoms Up Book 3.5 Jessica and Joseph Short

Renew, Book 4 (Jessica and Joseph)

Cocky Billionaire Boys

Cocky Catcher (Cocky Billionaire Boys Book 1)

Bossy Billionaire (Cocky Billionaire Boys Book 2)

The Fuertes Cartel

Stolen (The Fuertes Cartel Book 1)
Saved (The Fuertes Cartel Book 2)
Betrayed (The Fuertes Cartel Book 3)
<u>Carrington Cartel</u>
Torn: The Carrington Cartel Book 1
Claim: The Carrington Cartel Book 2
<u>Something</u>
Something Gained: A Romantic Comedy Book 1
Something Earned: A Romantic Comedy Book 2
<u>Pierce Motors</u>
Refuel: (Pierce Motors Book l)
Pressure: Pierce Motors Book 2)
<u>Summer Break</u>
Summer Nights: (Summer Break Book 1)
<u>TN Seal Security</u>
Aydin: Book 1
Nasir: Book 2
Nicco: Book 3
<u>Standalones</u>
Until Serena(HEA World Novel)
Temptation
She's All I Need
I Deserve His Love
Mutual Agreement
Scoring with Sadie
Exposed (A Bodyguard Novel)
Love Shorts:A Collection of Short Stories
Red Light District(A Fantasy Romance Short)

About the Author

KeKe Renée writes Sinful, Sexy, and Spicy Romances in Novelette, Novella, and Short Story form in genres ranging from Erotic, Paranormal, Contemporary, and Women's Fiction with HFN or HEA.

What's Next?

Want to know what happens next? Follow me at the links below to catch the next release.

Thank you so much for reading, and if you enjoyed the crazy ride and decided to leave a review, we'd truly appreciate the support. Reviews are the lifeblood of the publishing world. They're read, appreciated, and needed. Please consider taking the time to leave a few words on Goodreads or Bookbub.

Acknowledgments

I CAN'T MENTION ENOUGH the support and dedication of my author buddies for keeping me uplifted. My behind the scenes team of beta readers, editors, designers, and more. As a writer I continue to strive for the best, and I appreciate each and every one that reads my work. Without your continual feedback I wouldn't be on this path, letting doubts slip away.